FAMILY

OF

STRANGERS

A Gothic novel of Victorian Scotland where a young widow discovers that an unexpected legacy has turned her husband's unknown family away from her while a callous predator plotting her death wears a smiling face.

Janis Susan May

– Author's Revised Edition –

S~AB
SEFKHAT~AWBI BOOKS

Dedicated with all my love
to the memories of my wonderful parents,
Aletha Barrett May and Donald Wright May
and
to the most wonderful man in the world,
CAPT Hiram M. Patterson, USN/Ret

Copyright © 1984 by Janis Susan May

Originally published by Walker Publishing Company and
simultaneously in Canada by John Wiley & Sons Canada,
Limited, Rexdale, Ontario, 1984

Author's Revised Edition published by
Sefkhat-Awbi Books 2014

ISBN – 978-0-9857884-8-3

Books by Janis Susan May
electronic and/or paperback format

The Avenging Maid
The Fair Amazon
The Devil of Dragon House
Legacy of Shades
The Egyptian File
Inheritance of Shadows
Lure of the Mummy
Timeless Innocents
Welcome Home
Miss Morrison's Second Chance
Curse of the Exile
Echoes in the Dark
Dark Music
Quartet: Four Slightly Twisted Tales
Lacey
Passion's Choice
The Other Half of Your Heart

Books by Janis Patterson
electronic and/or paperback format

The Hollow House
Beaded to Death
Murder to Mil-Spec (anthology)

Books by Janis Susan Patterson
electronic and/or paperback format

Danny and the Dust Bunnies (childrens)

Chapter 1

The cold wind whipped around my ankles, riffling the hem of my dress and making the heavy serge of my cloak shudder over scuffed shoetops. Above us the sky was a leaden grey heavy with unshed rain, all too suitable for covering a small, poor churchyard and the yawning grave that was waiting like a hungry mouth to devour a simple wooden casket. Showing the truth of her good soul beneath a crusty exterior, Mrs. Morrison stood beside me at the burial of my so very new husband, just as she had stood behind Duncan and me a fortnight before when my mother had been buried. The raw earth of her grave, barely softened by the recent rains, lay humped in painful reminder next to where her all but unknown son-in-law would lie.

A work-roughened hand gripped my cold ones and slid them into the comforting warmth of her most prized possession, an aged fur muff of uncertain animal origin. "Poor babe," the landlady murmured huskily. "To be sure, it is an unhappy life you've had."

Unhappy? I had never thought of it that way,

but it is said that you never miss what you have never known. I suppose that is why when I am asked if my childhood were not a lonely and unhappy one I must stop and think before answering. Indeed, by the standards of the world it must have seemed so, with just my mother and myself, but I was content.

We had lived quietly, in a series of lodgings, and I was quite a big girl before I realized that the shabby rooms we inhabited were at a distinct variance with my mother's cultured ways and manners. No other child in our neighborhood had a mother who never screamed or drank, who spoke French as easily as English, or who was so fastidious about her—and my—appearance. Sometimes, while looking out the window at the happy, grubby urchins playing below, I would resent the fact that I had to study, to wear clean dresses, and was not allowed the run of the street with the other children. It was difficult playing so much indoors—until I became old enough to appreciate the escape to be found in books—for I had to stay in unless Mother could take me to the small park near our lodgings, and when she could not I had to be quiet, for it was understood that I should never disturb Mother at her work. When I became older I began to help her, copying manuscripts for a few pence per page in the flowing hand she had so laboriously taught me.

I have few memories of my father, which is to be expected, as I cannot recall his ever being around at any time past my fifth year. I remember a scent of tobacco, sweet and pungent, and a stronger odor, similar to that which issued from the grog shop on the corner. I remember being grabbed by two huge hands, called "Linnet, m'gel," swept through space as if flying, and held high in the air until I screamed from sheer terror. I remember laughter, but not very often. More often there were quarrels, hard words I could not understand that would leave Mother crying. Often in the mornings she was bruised and cut, but she tried valiantly to act as if nothing were out of the ordinary, and succeeded so well that I was much older before learning that this was not the normal order of things.

While very young I learned the necessity of economy. There never seemed to be enough money. Our rooms were shabby and in the poorest neighborhoods; our fires—when we had them—were always niggardly. Our clothes were plain and serviceable, without any decoration or frills, though to give Mother her due, I must say she went without herself to see that I had decent dresses—made with her own hands in the evening after the day's quota of manuscript had been copied. We ate frugally, though as well as we could afford, for Mother insisted on our keeping our health through an adequate diet. We could not afford the luxury of being sick.

Still, not all of Mother's precautions could protect her from the creeping weakness of consumption brought about by years of worry and unrelenting work. I was fifteen when she first became ill, and in the succeeding three years until her death our roles had gradually reversed, with me doing more and more of the copying work and she becoming progressively weaker and more dependent. It was a sign of her final capitulation that she sent me out alone to deliver and pick up manuscripts; in her ordered world young ladies of my tender years were not allowed out unescorted. In deference to Mother's feelings, I persuaded Mrs. Morrison, our landlady for the past two years, to accompany me whenever possible, but that starchy lady had business of her own to attend to and it became an accepted thing between us that in my reporting to Mother of our activities, Mrs. Morrison had chaperoned me, whether she did in fact or not. Perhaps I should feel remorse for putting my mortal soul in jeopardy with deliberate lies, but at the time my mother's peace of mind was paramount in my feelings. I have no reason to regret my decisions because it was on one of my solitary expeditions that I met Duncan MacLellan.

Our first meeting was hardly auspicious. I had been to the British Museum to deliver a completed manuscript to a funny little gentleman who gave Mother and me a great deal of business. Ironic now to think that I met Duncan because of a carelessly driven carriage—though there are enough of those in London at any given time as to be almost commonplace. I could not have guessed it to have had any especial significance. With the wide-eyed stare of a tourist, he had been more intent on the rising magnificence of the museum than the swirling traffic. I had seen the hurtling closed carriage bearing down on an unwary pedestrian and with more compassion than common sense rushed to fling myself against him, precipitating us both to an ungraceful and painful fall to the kerb, but out of the carriage's thundering path.

Our acquaintance began then, barely pausing at the level of friendship before developing into a warm and caring love. Mother, now so weakened that not even the unknown occasion of a gentleman caller could bestir her from her bed, was as quickly entranced by Duncan as I. Indeed, who could remain unaffected by the handsome charm and laughing blue eyes of Duncan MacLellan?

Mother was less pleased that he was a Scot, in London for a short time only on business matters, but pleased with both his breeding and his modesty about his landholdings. I did not like the venal appearance that Mother presented, quizzing Duncan so closely about his property and expectations, even though I was absent from the actual proceedings, but Duncan later told me he respected her acumen; she had had such a hard life, he explained, that it was only natural to wish something better for her daughter. His lands were respectably large, but brought in little income; generations of ill-management had fallen on his shoulders to rectify. Still, Duncan had a warm strength that made it easy to be comfortable with him, and so when he asked Mother for my hand after a courtship of mere days instead of respectable months or years, she happily gave her consent and blessing.

It was as if she had rid herself of a burden, and

therefore of life, for Mother died not two days later. Despite my objections, Duncan—aided by a sympathetic Mrs. Morrison—convinced me that it would be doing my mother no disrespect to marry quickly. She had blessed our union, and had worried about what would become of me after her death, never fully realizing that for the past few months I had taken care of her rather than she of me. Duncan and I should have to be wed anyway within a month, for then Duncan would have to return to his responsibilities at Kilayrnock; his arguments were very persuasive. I acceded to his wishes, and within a week Linnet Hudson had become Mrs. Duncan MacLellan.

Now Mrs. Duncan MacLellan, bride, had become a widow.

The service was over. Mrs. Morrison had led me back to the house and installed me in the knick-knack-filled closeness of her own parlor, fussed about with lap robes and hot bricks and tea, all the while keeping up a steady stream of chatter. I listened to her words with intent concentration, feeling that if I lost the thread of her conversation I should go flying out into the void.

"Such a tragedy," she clucked, pouring a generous dollop of top milk into my tea. "And him such a young man, too. Those dray drivers ought to be fined for the way they rush through the streets, even when there's no accident. Downright murderous they are!"

Such irony that Duncan—beautiful, loving Duncan—should have been brought into my life by an accident, and barely six weeks later taken from me by another. It outraged my sense of justice that the dray driver, no doubt hurrying through the narrow passage to meet his schedule, had neither stopped to give succor nor been apprehended. The police had been professionally sympathetic but unencouraging. I put my faith for just retribution in God alone, for the bobbies promised no help.

"And what are you going to do now, Miss Linnet?"

It would be unfair to Mrs. Morrison to say that her concern was prompted solely by a thought to her weekly rent, but she was a businesswoman. At the moment I had nothing beyond the few pounds which Duncan had given me; to start to find copywork again would take both time and energy. I had too much of the former empty, and too little of the latter.

Mrs. Morrison barely drew breath before launching another question, and I knew her first remark had been intended only as an opening. "You could write to that General Bellamy. He's your grandfather, after all."

How strange it had been to learn that I had a grandfather. Mother had never mentioned her family; she might have sprung full-blown into adulthood like Athena for all that she would say. It was only after her death, when I had taken on myself the painful task of sorting her few belongings and papers, that I had found she was the daughter of General Bellamy of Finchwood Hall, outcast when she defied parental decree and eloped with the handsome scoundrel who had been my father.

"No. Any man who would cut his own child off so completely would never acknowledge a grandchild. Besides, I am the daughter of the man he hated so. I have no claim on him, nor he on me." I stopped and took a deep breath. The idea came so quickly, so completely, that it must have been brewing in the back of my mind since that awful moment when the policemen apologetically told me of Duncan's death. "I shall go to Jura House."

Mrs. Morrison's cup stopped halfway between the saucer and her pursed lips. "To where?"

"Jura House. Duncan's home."

"All the way to Scotland to live among strangers? Foreigners, and most of them little better than savages from what I hear, no matter what the Queen thinks! Child, you must be touched! Have you a fever?" Knotted and arthritic fingers caressed my brow.

"Had Duncan lived, it would have been my home. I have not met his aunts nor brother, but they are now my family-in-law."

"But to Scotland! Alone! You are naught but a babe!"

It is amazing that in this modern year of 1880 there should still exist a prejudice against a female traveling alone across the city of London, let alone across the country. I determined not to let it bother me; my old life had been torn from me, so I would build a new one unhampered by antique attitudes and restrictions.

"I should think that my widow's weeds will act as sufficient deterrent to unwanted attentions, Mrs. Morrison. There is more than enough money for my passage, and at Jura House I can enjoy their hospitality while deciding on the future course of my life." In my mind's eye I built a comforting picture of welcome and relaxation in Jura House, from whose haven I could start again. "I shall go to Duncan's home."

Considering the frugality of my life in London, it should have been a simple matter to depart, but an assortment of delays kept me occupied the better part of a week. There was the disposal of such accumulated bits and pieces that I did not want to keep but that parting with proved to be an unexpected and painful wrench. I had to notify the police of my intention and destination, as the investigation into Duncan's death was still an open file, though I had no great hopes of its ever being solved. One of the pages from my last copying job had mysteriously become soaked, and as the author was out of town, I was called in to try and reconstruct the blurred and ruined prose.

All in all, it was five days after Duncan's funeral before the ever-stalwart Mrs. Morrison put me on the northbound train, giving me a box of sandwiches and fruit and a running string of advice about avoiding strangers and finding some respectable older woman as a traveling companion. I will not relate the account of my trip north, save that it was long, cold, and incredibly lonely. Duncan had spoken with love of his homeland, telling of the wild beauty of the mountains and moors, but I could see nothing save lonely emptiness so vast it rivaled that in my own heart.

Chapter 2

There were four windows in the dank little station of Kilayrnock, having between them thirty-two window panes. One of them was cracked. I had counted them several times in the last hours, trying to hide the hurt in my heart and to take my mind from how cold it was. The small fire in the stove was growing colder as it died naturally; obviously, after the last train of the night, the wizened little station-master would not leave a good fire to burn alone.

I had not been met. All the way from London my mind had rehearsed various scenes of meeting with Duncan's family, ranging from a wistful hope of a warm and loving welcome to a despairing fear of denunciation and rejection. It had never occurred to me that they would choose to ignore me altogether.

The stationmaster was a tiny gnome of a man, fully half a head shorter than I, but gnarled and strong as a storm-shaped oak tree. He wore trousers in the southern style, but made of some plaid whose design was mainly hidden by dirt and wear. A soft knitted cap, which I was later to call a tam-o-shanter, molded warmly about his ears and he seemed to be wrapped in an indeterminate number of shawls against the insidious and prying wind.

"So ye be Master Duncan's wife," he remarked for the third or perhaps fourth time. "Odd they no be coming to meet ye."

At first his conversation had been comforting, proof that I was not alone in the great dark void that was all I had seen of Scotland, but its gloomy tone and repetitiousness were fraying my already strained nerves. "Yes, it is. In such a wilderness I should hate to be abandoned. However, I suppose it is not unusual for telegrams to go astray?" I hated myself for the hopeful tone my voice took, as if longing for confirmation.

He seemed affronted at the word "wilderness," as well as what he took to be a slur against his ability. "Any telegrams that comes here I takes meself, lass."

"And do you remember mine?"

For a moment something flashed in the deeply buried eyes, then he shook his head. "Nay. I canna remember everything that passes my desk."

Although he spoke with the greatest conviction, I could not believe that there was such a volume of wire messages in this desolate area, nor that he could forget one of such local importance; Duncan had been well known in this area and the circumstances concerning his marriage and death should provide fodder for many years' gossip.

"Is there a carriage to be hired?" I asked suddenly. My purse was very slim, but Duncan had said that Jura House was not far from the Kilayrnock station, and I had to get there.

The gnome—for so I had begun to think of him—scratched his chin ruminatively. "Aye, Sandy McPherson sometimes rents his gig, but he's gone till Sabbath next."

My heart sank. "So there is no way for me to get to Jura House tonight."

"Nae short of walking. Better to take the late milker on to Dumfries."

His callousness aroused a streak of temper I had thought long vanquished. My besetting sin has always been to act before thinking, and any decision made in a storm of emotion is never quite rational. However, if I were to freeze to death I would rather it be in a struggle for attainment than sitting in a chilly stationhouse, and it would be difficult to convince me that the gnome would go out of his way to provide anyone with comfort and succor.

"Very well." I stood, straightening my cloak and reticule in the manner of a knight preparing for a battle. "I presume you can give me directions?"

He looked somewhat startled. "Sure, and ye won't be walking, miss!"

"Why not? And it is Mrs. —Mrs. MacLellan," I added waspishly. The creature must be feeble-minded, for I had impressed on him at least twice my name and title. "Apparently there is no other way to Jura House other than by foot. My late husband told me it was not far from the station. I have no intention of spending a cold and uncomfortable night when my home is but a short distance away."

"Aye, it is but three miles," he said much to my dismay. Three miles is not my idea of a short distance, but now my pride, fueled by anger, would not have protested had it been twice that.

"I shall leave my luggage here and send for it in the morning. Now . . . the way?" I asked haughtily.

Such a display of determination softened his attitude, for he repeated his directions twice to be sure of my comprehension. "Now, this road here goes to the valley. Ye goes along here to the second turning—there be a great stone pillar there with some sort of fantastical beastie carved on it. The dominie do say it be some kind of heathen demon. There ye turns left, and the drive to Jura House is a wee road to the left with a white gate. 'Tis powerful late, missus; would ye nae consider staying here til morn? I'll build ye a fire and ye can take the milk train to Dumfries where there be a proper hotel."

His abject change of manner should have made some impression on me, but I was too far gone in the high crest of emotion to notice subtleties. "When I am but a short walk from home? Nonsense."

Thirty minutes later his suggestion seemed to be rather simple and my own quixotic actions to be sheer madness. It was a clear night, cloudless and extremely cold, especially when the wind whistled through my totally inadequate town cloak. There was no moon, but the stars in brilliant abundance provided enough light to make out the shape of the road. My momentary and foolish flash of bravado had evaporated into the frigid air, to be replaced by a sense of dogged despair. Telegrams did get misdirected; there might even be some problem at Jura House that precluded their meeting me. Even if they had tried to contact me, reaching someone traveling on a train was a tricky business.

I plodded on, beating my arms to augment the warmth from my skimpy cloak. Luckily, my skirt was not so tight nor my bustle so large as to be the first stare of fashion, for had they been I would have been hard-pressed to do more than hobble. Duncan had insisted on buying me a new dress once he had become my husband, though out of deference to my late mother, it had been black. It was quite the most fashionable garment I had ever owned, and the thought of its hem dragging along the hard-packed road was distressing.

The stationmaster's directions were excellent, for the second turning off the high road was a smaller lane guarded by stone pillars. The stars did not give off enough life to discern the shape of the "fantastical beastie" carved thereon, but my curious fingers, only slightly less chill than the unyielding stone, felt something resembling a mythical griffon, a creature half eagle and half lion; it was hardly a comforting image to think of on such an inhospitable night.

The lane was smaller and rougher; I was compelled to go more slowly to keep my balance on the uneven road. Even the faint starlight was blocked by the interlacing arch of trees. It must have been due to my concentration on staying upright that I did not hear the hoofbeats until they were almost on me. Had I been more comprehending and less uncomfortable, I would have questioned anyone who put his horse at such a pace down a rough and rutted lane, but at the moment my sole concern was that there was someone in this world of dark and cold besides myself.

"Help!" I cried. "Please stop."

There was a clear space ahead, made reasonably bright by the absence of overhanging trees. I dashed for it, fearful lest my dark garb make me into a shadow invisible in the night.

Then the astonishing thing happened, something that shocks me still to this day. I stood in the faint starlight, waving my arms as one would flagging down a train, and just as mindless as a train, the rider came straight towards me without slackening speed. My last conscious action was one of sheer survival instinct; I leapt into the ditch, but not so quickly that my head was not cruelly struck. I sank into the weeds and into unconsciousness simultaneously, not even hearing the drumming of fading hoofbeats.

* * * * *

My head hurt, my entire being hurt, and in a way I was glad of it, for it showed me still to be alive. With an unknown instinct directing my cloudy consciousness, I slithered like some swamp creature through the weeds of the ditch back onto the lane; that tiny distance, measurable in inches, cost me more in energy and pain than the entire long walk from the station. I knew I had been unconscious and that I would soon faint away again, but no matter what, I could not simply wait for the Angel of Death to claim me as his own.

I lay in the rutted road, the gaudy profusion of stars above me, hovering between painful awareness and the smoky region of unconsciousness, when once again the ground beneath me vibrated from the impact of hooves. It was over, I thought. Now I could not move even to save my life, for my bones had turned to ice from which my flesh shrank with no power nor will to move. I drowsed, aware, yet as one dead.

The hoofbeats stopped not a yard away from my prostrate form. There was a jangling of harness and a creak of leather as a startling apparition spread his dark wings and swooped toward me. My mind murmured a prayer consigning my soul to God's mercy that my lips could not. Our Father, Who Art in Heaven . . .

"Well, Annie," said a voice too intensely masculine and disapproving to have anything to do with the celestial regions, "what have you done to yourself now? If you must sample the whiskey, at least do it at your croft, where you won't be a menace to traffic or yourself. What the Devil . . . !" His voice changed from disapproving to angry amazement as strong hands turned me where my face was visible in the faint light.

"You aren't Old Annie," the voice challenged roughly, even as surprisingly gentle fingers sketched the outline of my face. "You've been hurt. Now where did you come from, so late at night in the middle of nowhere?" Softly he brushed away the tangled wreckage of my coiffure. "A beauty, too, but you won't last long if I don't do something about you right away."

It was humiliating to be talked to and touched without even the opportunity of a reply, but my sullen body refused to heed any command of my mind. Barely on the edge of consciousness, I could only lie and hear myself discussed, a state of affairs my strong will could not tolerate.

"Did you," I whispered with painful effort, "come back to finish the job?"

I was lifted in strong arms. The dreaded

wings were naught more than a heavy woolen cloak, and in short order it was wrapped around me, pressing me close to the warmth of his body. He asked several questions in that quick, authoritative manner and even shook me, but I was floating in clouds of grey and incapable of answering; then, at last, unknowing.

The motion of the horse brought me back to a vague state of consciousness. He was galloping at a reckless speed, with me limp across his saddle bow and clasped tightly to his chest, cocooned in his left arm and the thick cloak. Oddly enough, though I was immobile and barely conscious, I had never been so aware of my senses. A variety of scents flooded my nostrils; damp wool and ironed linen, talc and bay rum, a certain pleasant muskiness that must be the scent of the man. The rough wool was pleasant against my left cheek, as was the finer weave of his sleeve on the other side of my face. And ... how can I state this without giving permanent offense to both delicacy and taste, yet still convey the sensation that coursed through me? Until then my only experience and contact with the male physique had been Duncan, who despite his excellence of character had been scarcely more than my height and not dissimilarly slender in build. Now my cheek rested on an arm only slightly less soft than a metal bar. The body against which I reposed was that of a giant or an athlete as is sometimes seen in ancient sculpture, firm and hard and unyielding as the marble itself.

The horse slithered to an uncomfortably quick halt, and then there was an impression of a number of people, all come in answer to the rescuer's bellow, a gigantic sound that seemed to rumble forth as if coming up from his shoes.

"Sir!" A groom ran forward to grab the horse's bridle. His voice had the same soft burr as the stationmaster's, rather than the hard edge of my rescuer's.

"Take Crusader to the stables, then saddle Brutus and ride for the doctor. He's to come at once, or this lady may die." Effortlessly my giant swung down from the saddle without ever loosing his hold on me. I am taller than the average female and no stretch of the imagination could ever term me to be of delicate frame, yet he carried me as if I were thistledown. It felt as if I were flying—or perhaps I was, for the world was full of grey clouds . . .

* * * * *

"And how do you feel now?"

I took a long breath and looked back into the kindly eyes of the doctor. "Alive, that's good enough, I suppose."

"Praise be," said the stolidly imperturbable housekeeper, Mrs. Wright. She had been a tower of strength—a term much abused, but here highly deserved—during my struggles back to consciousness and terror when the doctor had said my face should have to be stitched. The ordeal had not been as bad as my horrors would have painted it, but Mrs. Wright had been there, unruffled by such dramatics in her respectable household. I suppose my trust in her was due to the fact that she was most reminiscent of Mrs. Morrison, though lacking that lady's tart and acerbic tongue. There was even a dim memory that during the time of my extremity, I had gone so far as to call her by that name.

It was her nightgown that I wore now, a humble sort of garment, totally at variance with the splendor of the bedchamber in which I lay. Never in my life had I seen such a room outside of picture books. Silk covered the walls and hung in swaths from the tester; the mattress was as soft as one would imagine a cloud. A fire, scarcely smaller than a major conflagration, burned in the huge hearth; my eyesight was slightly blurred, but there was no question that the mantel bosses bore the same griffon that had adorned the stone pillar marking the beginning of the lane. Had I not hurt so abominably in so many parts of my person, I would have sworn that I had died and gone to Heaven.

"Well, there's no danger of your dying," the doctor said, as if in echo of my thoughts. "At least not now, since you didn't lie exposed to the air all night. If Mr. Fordyce hadn't found you, you probably would have been dead by morning. As it is, you will probably be damnably sore for a time . . . it will take at least a fortnight for those bruises to fade. You'll probably be prone to headaches for a while; I'll leave some powders you can take. Now I want you to get plenty of rest and take it easy, and you'll be right as a trivet. I'll be right back in a week or so and see to taking out your stitches."

"Very well, but how soon shall I be ready to travel? I don't want to be any more of a charge to Mr. . . . Fordyce, is it? . . . than I already have. I must go home."

The doctor paused in the act of putting all his evil-looking instruments back into the squat black bag. "Home? You can't be traveling any distance for a while yet. You aren't from around here, I believe."

How complicated things become! "Well, in a way. I was on my way home for the first time . . . I'm Linnet Hudson . . . No, I'm Mrs. Duncan MacLellan now and I live at Jura House."

The doorway was filled by a muscular masculine form.

"The Devil you say!" snarled Simon Fordyce.

Chapter 3

It may be most improper for a lady to receive alone in her bedchamber a gentleman who is neither her husband nor her physician, but I am honest enough to admit that after the first few moments in the sole company of Mr. Simon Fordyce I felt neither shame nor discomfiture. As he remorselessly shooed the doctor and an indignantly proper Mrs. Wright from the room, I had a chance to study him.

He proved not to be the giant of my wandering imagination, but he was tall and muscularly built. Though he had discarded the great dark cloak, he still wore his travel-stained riding clothes, which made him look strangely out of place in this elegant room. How can I describe him when mere words can never catch the energy nor the magnetism of this man? Forthrightly described, Simon Fordyce could have been almost anyone. His hair was a dark brown, worn carelessly back and longer than the current style, as if he neglected having it cut. His skin was tanned from contact with the weather, but originally it would seem to have been fair rather than swarthy. His features were extremely handsome and strongly defined, but once one saw his eyes, all else faded away in the glare of their blue fire. They were visionary's eyes or, to put it more fancifully, the eyes of some antique god or demon—fully in keeping with the griffon symbol that decorated his house. Their stare was hypnotic.

I looked away.

"Now that you've had a chance to study me, do I conform to your idea?" he asked mildly, pulling a heavy desk chair to my bedside as if it had been weightless.

"Since I have never heard of or seen you before this evening, I can scarcely have any idea of you or your appearance," I answered in kind.

"Come now. You mean, Mrs. MacLellan, that your husband has never mentioned me to you? Nor his family?"

"No. Duncan talked very little about his home and I do not remember your name being mentioned. As for his family ... I have never met them and indeed have heard but little of them." His startled exclamation was in itself a question, so I went on, haltingly at times, to tell him of my pitifully short marriage. I had not meant to make a bid for his sympathy, but so many threads of my life were interwoven that by the time all was explained he knew of my recent double bereavement and I was weeping helplessly.

Before I could recover my composure he was on the bed beside me as if it were the most natural thing in the world, cradling my head on his shoulder as he swabbed my eyes with his handkerchief. It smelt of bay rum. He offered no words of sympathy, for which I respected him. No words yet invented could have comforted me then. When my sobs had subsided he pressed a glass into my hands and ordered me to drink it all; I did so unquestioningly, choking at the earthy-tasting draught of pure fire.

"What was that?"

"The local whiskey. There . . . that brought some color back into your face."

"I feel as if I could burst into flames at any moment. What horrid stuff!"

He laughed easily and moved off the bed back into his chair. I applied his handkerchief to my eyes, streaming now from the whiskey rather than emotion.

"There are those who would disagree with you. It is very highly sought after. Now, Mrs. MacLellan, if it would not be too painful for you, I should like to ask you some questions."

"Of course. What would you like to know?"

"When I found you on the lane you seemed to come to consciousness for a moment. You looked up at me and said something about my coming back to finish the job. What did you mean? What happened out there?"

I could not suppress a shudder. For a moment it all came back— the dark, the cold, the hoofbeats drumming on the ground in some obscene pattern of thundering death . . . As calmly as possible I told him of the incident, keeping back only my semi-consciousness as he carried me homeward.

He glowered, the blue eyes all but shooting sparks. "So you thought me capable of killing a woman, and by such cowardly means! Hardly flattering."

"I did not know you, Mr. Fordyce."

"True," he said, and the hard light paled. "I apologize. Though it sounds like something your husband's family would say."

The bitter edge in his tone sliced at me. It was as decided an insult to those of my husband's blood as I should ever hear, but I could offer no outrage nor contravention, since I knew them not.

"There are," he added with an air of understatement, "bad feelings between your husband's family and me." Gently his finger traced the outline of stitching along the side of my head. "This is exactly the sort of thing they would attribute to me, along with bringing fire, flood, and windstorm as well as dancing with the Devil's daughter."

"Duncan mentioned no ill-feelings . . ."

Mr. Fordyce smiled, transforming his face to an amazing handsomeness. "I can well understand why a man on his honeymoon would not wish to discuss troubles."

"But we talked so much about the valley, and his plans for the place . . . He was a very gentle man, Mr. Fordyce," I added with unusual emphasis. Somehow it seemed important to convince him of that.

"Indeed. I knew your husband, Mrs. MacLellan,

and quite frankly, he was the best of the bunch at Jura House." He cleared his throat with a deprecating cough that in another man would have passed for embarrassment. "I cannot say I am happy that you are going to live among those people."

"They are my family now," I said with dignity. It sounded pitiful, and I hated it.

"Is there no one else to whom you could turn? No other relative or friend in London, perhaps?"

I would not play on his emotions by telling him the only person in this world who cared if I lived or died was a former landlady. That was too shame-provoking! "I prefer to stay here, in Scotland. I hate to trespass further on your hospitality, but could you arrange transport for me to Jura House?"

He frowned. "So I cannot convince you otherwise? So be it. I will take you there myself—and a fine fuss that will cause! — but only on the morrow. I sent a groom to explain the circumstances, so they won't be expecting you. Besides, it is very late now and the doctor said that you must rest."

"I didn't stop to think . . . What time is it?"

'Just past one. Here. This is a sleeping draught the doctor left for you. I want you to drink every drop of it." He pressed a fizzing glass into my hand, his strong fingers molding mine to hold it.

I drank. It was vile, but he stood there to make sure I finished it, then took the glass from my numb grasp. Only one in the morning. It seemed as if I had lived and died innumerable times, but it had only been a few hours.

"I'll leave the mantle light burning so you won't be frightened waking up in a strange place," he murmured. "Call if you need anything . . ." His final benediction echoed gently in my mind as I faded into oblivion.

Simon Fordyce was as good as his word. Though he did try once more to dissuade me from my chosen plan of action, on seeing that I was firm he gave every assistance. After a hearty breakfast in bed, I was assisted to dress by the kindly Mrs. Wright, who made no secret of her disapproval of my destination. My clothes looked as good as they ever had, having been cleaned and refurbished during the night as if by genies. Although I was tired and dizzy by the time I was dressed, there was also a sense of anticipation. Today I would meet Duncan's family.

The morning was clear and flooded with the sparkling magic light of which Duncan had spoken so lovingly. I could understand his fascination for it now, the liquid blue light touching the hills and trees with a curious glow not entirely of this earth. The land rolled away in a giant patchwork of green and grey and gold and lilac, traced with hedges of gorse. In the spring, the thick bushes would be solid with yellow and purple blossoms, but now in the autumn they were heavy brown.

"It is beautiful," I murmured.

"And becomes even more so," Mr. Fordyce replied, his voice husky with a sound like passion.

Clicking to the horses, we proceeded away down the drive at a sedate pace.

Over my protests he had carried me from the elegant bedchamber, down the stairs, and through the hallway to where the light carriage had waited by the front door. It was from there that I bade farewell to Mrs. Wright, who begged me to remember her and offered her aid any time I should need her. Although it was a kindly gesture, I could not help wondering as we drove away just what sort of people they thought Duncan's family were! Perhaps that was one of the reasons I had been brought to this desolate northern country, to make peace between Duncan's people and those who held hard thoughts towards them. It was quite a romantic notion that filled a need within me, a desire to do something wonderful in my husband's name, something he doubtless would have done himself had he been spared.

"You look a bit flushed," Mr. Fordyce commented. "Are you sure you feel up to this trip? It's a good five miles there by road."

"It's only excitement. I feel perfectly fine." It was a lie, for I ached miserably from the top of my head down, but how wonderful it would be to recuperate in my own home, lovingly attended by Duncan's family. They would be able to explain how my arrival had gone unmet, and everything would be fine.

"There used to be a road directly from the Castle to Jura House and one didn't have to take the long way around the lane," he said easily. "Less than two miles. I wish it were open so that you wouldn't have to get so tired."

So did I, but I would not admit to such weakness. "What became of it?"

"The MacLellans put a stone wall across it."

"Why?"

He looked at me searchingly. One could easily drown in his blue eyes. "Did your husband tell you nothing?"

"Not about feuds or stone walls. He talked about the people of the valley and his hopes for them and the beauty of each season . . ." For a moment Duncan's voice sounded in my ears as he spoke lovingly of the colors and scents of his homeland, and hot tears scalded my eyes. I took the proffered handkerchief—mine was buried at the bottom of my reticule—and wiped my face. "He told me nothing of anything ugly."

"No, I don't suppose Duncan MacLellan would. I guess I had better, though be careful what you say around his family, for if they hear that I told you they'll say it is all lies. If you had come as the bride of a MacLellan from an earlier generation, you would have been home last night."

"The Castle?" I overlooked the possible slur on Duncan and looked at him with interest. If I were going to make a success of my new life here, I would be better prepared the more information I had, though it did seem perilously close to gossiping.

"Yes, it was the MacLellan seat—in this part of

the country, at least—for generations." His face scowled until I wondered that I should have ever thought it handsome. "Your late husband's grandfather was a scoundrel and a gamester. He lost the Castle over a horserace."

I was appalled. I had not seen much of the structure, but it had appeared to be palatial both in size and elegance. The total waste of such beauty for the accursed practice of wagering was dreadful. From somewhere within my mind there came the memory of an old quarrel between my parents, little chunks of conversation, words like "gambling again" and "a gentleman's occupation." A remembered feeling of distaste made me shudder.

"How sublimely foolish. And what did you wager against it?"

His frown deepened. "I didn't. I'm no gamester, beyond a few friendly hands for token stakes. I bought the house from the man who won it; also, it seems, I bought the neighborhood enmity as well."

"How unfair."

"You should be in quite a position to comment on the unfairness of life, Mrs. MacLellan. Are you cold?"

"No," I replied through stiff lips. "I'm fine."

We drove in silence for quite a while. My smiling and considerate host of the evening before had disappeared, leaving behind a scowling stranger whom I found intimidating. Though he drove slowly, the motion of the carriage made my head ache; where the doctor had stitched the open wound now hurt abominably. It would have been so comforting to lie down; oh, to reach Jura House and some peace.

"Do you recognize this place?"

I looked around. The country lane was rutted and lined with weed-choked ditches, in turn bordered by a shabby-looking fence. Not far ahead tall and graceful trees rose in mutual splendor to form an archway through which the clotted sunlight dappled the road. Starlight alone would never be strong enough to penetrate that leafy bower.

"How normal it all seems. It hardly looks frightening or sinister at all."

He smiled, but it was thin and unwarming. With a flick of his wrist he started the carriage again—when had it stopped?—and after turning, we followed the lane to a somewhat dilapidated gate, hanging open on sprung hinges. Here we turned into an even more ill-kept lane, one so rutted that Mr. Fordyce was forced to pull back to a walk in order to keep from jostling us to pieces.

"I'm sorry if this hurts your head," he said, deftly steering the pair around a murderous pothole. "This seems to have deteriorated since I last came down it."

My teeth were gritted and my thoughts shamelessly filled with the comforts of my elegant bedchamber at the Castle. Once more I had brought difficulties down on my head by my impetuosity.

"What is the matter? Why doesn't someone see to its upkeep?"

"That, my dear Mrs. MacLellan, is something you'll have to ask your relations. This is the drive to Jura House." His voice was flat and strained. "I want to tell you something before we reach the house. Although your husband and I were hardly friends, I was not his enemy, despite what spiteful and malicious gossips say. And no matter what anyone says, I do not wish to be your enemy. Do you understand that?"

His gaze was compelling. At that moment such was his magnetism that I would have trusted him with the world, had it been in my power to give. Bereft of speech, I nodded despite the cost to my aching head.

"The hospitality of the Castle is open to you at any time, Mrs. MacLellan, and for any reason, whether I am there to act as host or not. If you should ever feel frightened . . ." His words trailed away, and many times in the future I would wonder what might have been spared had he continued speaking. Instead he pointed with the whip. "There is Jura House."

To one raised in the poorer sections of London with never more than a set of rooms to call home, the sight of Jura House should have been overwhelming, but after the magnificence of the Castle it was something of an anticlimax.

Built some centuries before in a sturdy and uncompromising style, at first glance Jura House had the air of a contented farmhouse with no artificial graces about it, but the closer one came the more evidences of neglect became obvious. The liquid sunshine gleamed dully off filthy mullioned panes and shamefully displayed the flaking plaster and rotting beams. Bushes untrimmed for so long that they resembled small forests in their own right clustered about, choking the house. It looked almost deserted except for a plumy wisp of smoke rising from one broken chimney pot.

My thoughts must have been writ plain across my face—Mother always told me I was incapable of dissembling—for a sour smile cracked Mr. Fordyce's darkened face. The sympathetic and kindly cavalier of the night before might have been only a fever dream of my own imagination, so different were my memories of my rescuer from the realities of my current companion.

"You're right. It is quite a comedown, and they've never forgotten it. Not much longer, Mrs. MacLellan; can you bear it? You're white as a sheet."

I fought back waves of dizziness, and though the swelling on the left side of my face would permit only a lopsided smile, I made it as brave a one as could be imagined. "I will be all right, Mr. Fordyce."

"You are an amazing woman," he murmured half under his breath, and it could have been my imagination, but it seemed that his exhalation of breath formed a counterfeit of my own Christian name, "Linnet."

To be honest, I have no clear memory of the last few hundred yards' trip to Jura House, nor of the enigmatic Mr. Fordyce's strong arms lifting me down with consummate tenderness and care from the carriage. I do remember the stained and cracked plaster that surrounded the weather-worn door and the faint though unmistakable stale smell—well known to anyone who has lived in lodgings for any length of time—of poverty and dirt that came flooding out when the door was opened.

I had no time to reflect on my surroundings, however, for the female who opened the door commanded all my attention, as she would have had we been in the centre of the Strand at midday. Middle-aged, middling tall, and close to scrawny, she could have been a man masquerading in petticoats had it not been for the length and luxuriousness of her grey hair, whose chignon a lace cap strained to cover. Her features, though not displeasingly arranged, wore an expression that would have stopped a belligerent bulldog in its tracks. I knew at this first look that even though this woman was my late Duncan's blood aunt, my aunt-in-law and my closest relative in the world save the grandfather who had repudiated both my mother and me, I could never – and never would be permitted to -- call her by any intimate familial appellation.

"Good day, Miss MacLellan," Mr. Fordyce said with easy courtesy. "You see I have delivered your niece-in-law as promised."

"We appreciate your kindness, Mr. Fordyce," she replied stiffly, as if the words were glass and cut her mouth as she spoke. To me she was more direct, even as she looked at me as she would have encroaching vermin. "Why did you not let us know that you were coming? We would have met you, and none of this foolishness about falling in the lane would have happened."

I was all too conscious of Mr. Fordyce's strong arm cradling mine, bracing me, to be entirely decorous and proper. The scent of his bay rum enveloped me like a cloud.

"I did wire . . ." I murmured, but my escort's tone, though softly spoken, drowned me out.

"Mrs. MacLellan has had a long journey and a serious injury. Might I suggest that our conversation be carried on inside, where she might be comfortably seated?"

Her strong features frozen, Miss MacLellan wordlessly swung the door wider and, assisted by Mr. Fordyce's steady arm, I stepped over the worn sill and onto the uneven flags of the hallway. It was dark in here, but even in the poor light I could see a lack of cleanliness that would have sent my poor mother into a fit.

"Is she here? Does she look like her picture?" Another voice, but lighter and carrying something of a smile, issued from the dark hole that I could only surmise was a doorway until she confirmed my suspicions by stepping through, looking anxiously at the copy of my wedding picture in her hands.

It had been a shameful extravagance, that

wedding photograph, but Duncan had insisted having one taken to send home to his aunts and brother; "so they can see what a beautiful girl I married," he had laughed lovingly. Now I was glad of it, for I had no other representation of my late loved one, but my thoughts were far away from the images in cardboard that she held.

The second aunt emerged, a softer, rounder, somehow blurred copy of her sister, but dressed in purple and frayed lace instead of the harsh black her sibling wore. There was another difference as well. The Miss MacLellan who had first appeared at the door seemed never to have smiled in her life, while the other, the one who held the photograph, seemed to have a simper permanently affixed to her lips.

"Oh, she is the image of her photograph! How lovely you are, my dear! What a pity this can't show the lovely brown of your hair. I vow, it is as soft-looking as the burn water in the fall!"

"These are your late husband's aunts," Mr. Fordyce murmured. "Miss Agatha and Miss Jessie MacLellan. They are twins."

That should have prepared me for what happened later, but I was still bedazzled by Miss Jessie's onrushing spate of words.

"But dear child, your face! We were not told that it was such a serious injury . . . You must be careful, you know, for we wouldn't want such a pretty face as yours to be scarred . . . How awful! It's good that Dougal is back from Edinburgh so he can look after you . . ."

A new voice entered the scene, one that snapped my head around with painful rapidity.

"Indeed, Linnet, we had no idea you had been so severely injured. What on earth happened?" asked my husband Duncan, reaching out toward me as I fell.

Chapter 4

For the second time in as many days I had awakened from unconsciousness in a strange bed, though this chamber showed none of the grace and elegance of the one at the Castle. Small and low-ceilinged, it possessed only one window and the plaster walls were thickly adorned with generations of candle soot. I carefully shifted position, feeling every lump and seam of the mattress against my bruised body. I had no memory of being undressed and put to bed in this stiff flannel nightgown, nor indeed any memory of aught since the hallway flagstones had rushed up to meet me, yet I was certain that it had been in Simon Fordyce's enfolding arms that I had been brought upstairs, his voice that had spoken out for my welfare.

When I had awakened, though, he was gone, I was stuffed into this abominably scratchy nightdress and brought a tray containing an indifferent lunch.

"Are you finished?" The face that was peeking around the door wore a lace cap.

"Yes—Miss Jessie?" I answered hesitantly.

She bustled into the room, her silly smile firmly

in place as she lifted the tea tray from my knees. "Yes! How quick you are! But you didn't eat much of this tasty luncheon. Shame on you, Linnet!"

In the face of such caring concern, it was impossible to tell her that the tasty luncheon she extolled had been largely inedible. Mother and I had ever been short of money, but our food was as nutritious and appealing as could be managed; nothing had ever been as execrable as the tray Miss Jessie had held hoveringly against my first return to consciousness, prepared to spoon soup into me the moment my mouth was opened. Only Miss Agatha's sharp summons had prevented her and left me to my own devices.

"I wasn't very hungry."

She placed the tray on a rickety table and returned to sit by my bed, eyeing me for all the world like a child with a new toy. "Now that's something you'll have to get over, Linnet. You must eat to keep up your strength and get well. You gave us an awful fright just keeling over like that, and in front of that horrible Fordyce man, too."

"Duncan never told me he and Dougal were twins. It was such a shock . . ."How could I describe in sterile words that awful moment when it seemed that the man whose mangled body I had buried in London had magically reappeared in Jura House, whole and hearty? Like any good Christian woman I believed in the blessings of Our Lord and the reassurance of the Resurrection, but that had been unnatural, uncanny, somehow tinged with evil . . .

Soft fingers, pudgy and pale, patted my tense hand. "Of course, child. Don't you fret. We're your family now, and we know all about your problems and you about ours."

I wanted to say that wasn't true, that I knew nothing of their problems, that Duncan had left me criminally in the dark, but the door opened to the scowling face of Miss Agatha and insensibly the room seemed to darken.

"So you're awake still, are you? How do you feel?" It was a challenge, not an inquiry about my welfare.

"I feel better, thank you."

"She hardly ate any of her lunch, Aggie. She must eat so she can get well." Miss Jessie's voice, though light and youthful, was strained with artifice.

"You cannot afford to be a picky eater, Linnet. We must be grateful for what we have." Miss Agatha's tone was bitter.

"We must be grateful that that old besom in the kitchen has not yet poisoned us," Dougal said lightly as he stepped into the room. "I cannot but believe that she took her training under the Borgias. Well, dear sister Linnet, you begin to look more like the beautiful girl my brother so lovingly described in his letters. I came to see if you felt up to some genteel conversation and find that you are holding a reception in your chamber!"

His gentle raillery brought a smile and giggle to

Miss Jessie's vacuous features, but shattered to nothing against Miss Agatha's graven expression. That worthy lady merely gave a snort of disdain, and with an all but snarled command to Miss Jessie, left the room with her sister in her wake.

Only those who have loved and lost will appreciate the Gethsemane I suffered as my dead husband's twin crossed the room to sit at my side. In features and form they were indeed identical; the curling mop of unruly chestnut hair, the golden eyes, and the juxtaposition of an almost femininely delicate mouth above a granite-edged jaw. With searing pain I remembered the touch of those lips, the embrace of those slender arms. Yet it was not those but others that were buried and lost to me forever.

"We are . . . were very like," Dougal said, and I agreed.

They were very like, and yet in a way very unlike. Though the outer shells were made from an identical mould, there was something indefinable that differentiated them, something that on calm reflection and study—though it had no proper name—would make it possible to distinguish the one from the other no matter the circumstances. I cannot describe this phenomenon nor its causes, but on deeper study, Dougal MacLellan was as different from my own dear Duncan as chalk from cheese. The spiritualists so much in vogue now in London would doubtless ascribe it to an aura or some other equally outlandish-sounding thing and they might be right; I only knew that I would never again mistake my dead husband for his brother.

"He was the elder," Dougal was saying, "by three and a half hours. It might as well have been three and a half years. The poor old boy got all the responsibility for the entire family, this falling-down old ruin, everything. Poor sot."

Such cavalier treatment of his heritage snagged at something within me. "He wished to rebuild it, to make the whole valley prosper. That was his dream."

"I know all about his dream. Used to preach it to me by the hour. I could never convince him of its impossibility."

Often I had heard Duncan mourn the fact that his brother did not share his hopes for the future of the valley. "And now it is yours. What are you going to do with it?"

"I suppose it is," Dougal murmured, as if the idea had not occurred to him before. "I would have had it otherwise, please believe that, but I suppose I must go ahead with my own dream now."

I watched the play of thought in those golden eyes, so painfully like and yet so unlike those I had loved. "And that is?"

"To restore the House of MacLellan to its former glory," he said with an intensity of feeling that was frightening.

The next day, in the disgracefully neglected and over-grown garden, I questioned Dougal further.

I reclined in a chair pulled from the parlor, feeling the healing intrinsic in the clear air of the Lowlands. The morning was crisp with the approaching autumn, but a heavy shawl pressed on me by Miss Jessie held any chill at bay.

"You said something about the House of MacLellan yesterday, just before I slept again. I thought in Scotland you had clans. Are you now head . . . the Laird, I believe . . . of the MacLellans?"

Dougal smiled lazily. "Our dear Victoria has been responsible for a number of misconceptions about Scotland, mostly about the clans. I fear that the clan system was smashed forever during the doomed rebellion of 1745, and in any case our branch of the family would be considered far too obscure for any sort of distinction. I must admit to smaller dreams . . . To rebuild the crofts, make the farms what they were before the clearances . . ." Noting my look of confusion, he paused.

"In the early part of this century, Linnet, great parts of the Highlands were swept clear of crofters—farmers—to raise sheep. We are not part of the Highlands, and the clearances were fairly mild around here, but the MacLellan land holdings were all but wiped out. Sheep do not do well in this country."

"But," I countered, using Duncan's oft-repeated argument, "isn't farming on a scale to be profitable in modern times impractical on this land?"

Something flashed in the depths of those golden

eyes and died. "I see Duncan managed to inculcate you with his heresies."

"Heresies?"

"To our tradition. The MacLellans have always been gentlemen of the land. Duncan had come too much under the influence of that damned usurper. That must be our first goal—to oust him!" His voice had died to a mere whisper. He leaned against the crumbling masonry of the wall enclosure, looking out over the rolling land with an expression usually reserved for lovers. As far as he was concerned, I was not there.

"Who?"

"That man who stole the Castle!"

"Mr. Fordyce?" I asked, startled. He had said that the relations between the two houses were strained, but nothing to indicate that such passions were involved. "He said he bought it."

"He would. Do not mistake me, dear Linnet, I am glad that he was so felicitously disposed as to come to your rescue, but it will make it difficult for you to see him for the villain he is instead of a kindly knight." The handsome face crumpled to an ugly mask. "Thief!"

"But he said he bought it . . ." I murmured. I had never suspected such intricacies in this strange homecoming. Perhaps Mrs. Morrison had been right after all.

"He would! Shall I tell you the true story? I hate to destroy the romantic picture you have built up of your gallant rescuer, but the man is a scoundrel."

A scoundrel? I thought back to those scowling features, that intense energy burning in blue eyes so full of strength . . . Yes, Simon Fordyce might well be a scoundrel, and a villain as well, but I should have a hard time believing it.

"I thought your grandfather lost the Castle."

Dougal smiled, and for a moment all resemblance to Duncan vanished. "Fordyce primed you well, didn't he? Yes, our dear grandfather was a gambling fool and he did lose the Castle over a horserace ; however, the wager was with one of his oldest friends, a man we had never had any reason to mistrust until Simon Fordyce came on the scene.

"You see, Linnet, according to the rules of honor, the man who loses a piece of property is to be given the first option to purchase it should it ever be sold. Old Man McPhail promised my father that he would have the right to buy the Castle back. Because of that promise, every ha'penny that could be scraped together was put aside for the repurchase of the Castle."

"What happened?"

"Simon Fordyce happened. He came looking for land, saw the Castle, and got friendly with Old Man McPhail, who broke both his word and the codes of honor when he sold it to him! But we got him, Linnet; it's a stalemate. The MacLellans own the land he needs, and we'll never sell."

"But doesn't the Castle have any land?"

"Just a few acres." He dismissed them with a contemptuous wave of his hand. "Never enough for a decent crop."

There was no answer to that, so I lay back and closed my eyes, to open them again only moments later when my hand was gently touched. Again there was the momentary shock when my gaze made contact with the externals of curly hair and golden eyes, and the inevitable disappointment when I beheld the substance rather than the surface of the man.

"Are you well? Would you prefer to go indoors?"

"No, it is so beautiful out here. I see now why Duncan loved this country so much. The light is incredibly beautiful . . . it changes all the time."

Dougal moved from his seat on the coping to a spot beside me, setting the chrysanthemums to showering petals on the warped brick walk. "You talk like an artist. Are you one?"

"I'm afraid not. That takes a talent with which I was not blessed, but thank Heaven I was gifted with an appreciation." An appreciation Duncan had fostered; how many times had I picked up or delivered manuscripts to the museum and walked right past the paintings in blind ignorance until Duncan had showed me the beauty captured in pigment and canvas?

"A pity you could not have seen the splendors of spring." Dougal's words were like a chilling shower. "Perhaps sometime in the future you can schedule a visit at that time of year."

I sat forward, absorbing the unvoiced message in his words. "I ask that you speak plainly. Am I not welcome here?"

To do him credit, a look of pain crossed his undeniably handsome features. "I did not say that, Linnet, and it hurts me that you could think such a thing. This was Duncan's home, and of course you are welcome here. However, you are a young woman and it is to be expected that after paying your grace visit here, after your mourning is over and your grief has healed somewhat, you will wish to return to the city, to your friends and your old life. This is a poor household, with little to interest a beautiful girl used to the amenities of life in London." He patted my hand again, his seraphic smile and kind words giving lie to their import.

This was to be no haven for me. They would tolerate me for a while, out of pity and politeness, but the dream I had held of a home where I would be welcomed and loved was nothing more than that. I should begin plans to leave this bitter refuge as soon as my face and body healed. Mrs. Morrison would find room for me, and doubtless I could once again build up my manuscript copying work. Such had been my life for many years, and I had been content, but could I go back after having had my life-long dream of a home and a husband realized for even such a short while?

Duncan, how could you go and leave me so alone?

By the time the sour-faced Miss Agatha called us in to a dinner of overdone mutton and underdone potatoes, I was in a fair taking of self-pity and in no state to hide my amazement at yet another ill-cooked meal. The dining room alone was enough to give anyone indigestion, being small and dark and airless; there was barely enough room between the walls and the table to scoot a chair, necessitating that the dishes be passed from hand to hand. There was no room for a servant to present the courses, even if Jura House possessed such an amenity, which from its state of uncleanliness I strongly doubted. A large and particularly repulsive picture of some dead birds dominated the wall before me, destroying my appetite quite as effectively as the food itself.

Miss Agatha gave me a look that contained volumes—none of them flattering—about finicky young women, but it was Miss Jessie, as greedy for conversation as she was for the thinly sliced mutton, who spoke first, barely giving us all time to be seated after a lengthy prayer.

"Oh, what a treat it is to have a visitor, especially one all the way from London! You must tell us everything about it, just everything! Did you go to the Opera? And the dances? Mother once had a friend who was presented to the Queen and her consort at a Royal Drawing Room . . ."

"Hush up and let Linnet eat her dinner, Jessie," Miss Agatha said without heat. She was shoveling in her food with a precision that might have rivaled any of the mechanical marvels with which our age is blessed. "Unless plain food is not good enough for her taste."

I had been wooling around a piece of meat, trying to cut it into a manageable bite, but my accursed temper could not help rising to such a challenge. Putting down my knife and fork, I stared at Miss Agatha, and the battle lines were drawn.

"I have never had anything but plain food in my life, Miss Agatha, and have never asked for anything else, but I do expect it to be edible. I don't know what kind of a fanciful idea you all have conceived of my being some sort of a London belle, but let me assure you that nothing could be further from the truth. My late mother and I made our living doing fair copies of manuscripts. We were desperately poor and never had more than two rooms to live in, but at least they were clean! Duncan never represented himself to be wealthy, but I must admit to find such a state of disorder in his house is shocking and disgusting. I know I am not welcome here, and . . ." My fine fury of words dissolved into a blubbering welter of emotion. Great slick tears slid from my eyes. Scrabbling in my pocket, I pulled out the large handkerchief Simon Fordyce had given me the day before, which I had forgotten to return.

Miss Agatha was immobile, staring at me as if I were some particularly fascinating form of insect life. Miss Jessie was making distressed cooing sounds, but would not speak in the face of her sister's anger.

"I am not surprised, miss, that Duncan should forget his duty to marry an heiress and choose you instead, for in a flashy way you are attractive, but I am shocked that he should so forget his breeding as to pick someone with such bad manners! Do you think we like living like this? Cramped into rooms made for a farmer's brood, rooms with no grace or style or symmetry? Do you think that we would voluntarily choose to be without the amenities of life due those of our birth?"

"I did not mean . . ." I began, but she went on as if she had not heard me.

"It is because of the family that we live like this . . . like peasants, so that every scrap possible can be put back to regain the Castle from that interloper for the rightful owners . . . the MacLellans!" Twin spots of high color glowed in her pale cheeks, giving her an incongruous clownlike appearance.

Such intense emotion was too much for me. Excusing myself, I all but ran up to the ugly bedchamber that had been Duncan's and where my luggage, at last brought from the station, awaited.

It is a sobering thought to see all of your life bound up into three cases and an antique tin trunk. No, not even that, for the smallest of the cases belonged to Duncan and contained the things he had taken to London. Mrs. Morrison had packed it the day of his death and I had not had the courage to open it since. I still could not, for the pain of seeing my late husband's effects combined with the pain of my situation was more than I could bear.

Before the light faded I was in bed, totally improbable plans for a new future coursing through my head in dreary succession. No one disturbed my solitude with any nighttime benediction, and I was firmly entrenched in sleep when the prowler came.

Chapter 5

A what? You are mad. That blow to the head must have deranged you," Miss Agatha said flatly. She did not even pause in the pouring of the breakfast tea. The pot was of silver and obviously old, but dented and, like the rest of the set, badly tarnished.

"A prowler? Oh, how exciting!" twittered Miss Jessie, faded eyes alight. "I don't recall us ever having a prowler. Dear Papa once shot a poacher in die wood north of the Castle, but that's not the same as a prowler . . ."

"Hush up, Jessie," ordered Miss Agatha. "The whole idea is ridiculous."

"Good morning, dear aunts . . . Linnet," Dougal said, cutting across all conversation. Handsomely clad in worn tweeds, he walked into the room proudly and once again that treacherous twinge of emotion plucked at my heart during the half-instant needed for recognition. Accepting his aunts' worshipful greeting as casually as he did his cup of tea, my brother-in-law took the seat at the head of the table. "Now, what is ridiculous?"

"Linnet," proclaimed Miss Agatha in a voice suitable to announcing that I had seen fairies in the bottom of the garden, "claims to have had a prowler during the night."

Dougal tried masterfully, but there was no way to disguise the amusement playing at the corners of his mouth. "A prowler? What makes you think so, Linnet?"

I was rapidly becoming upset at having my word treated so lightly. "I struggled with him, of course. He was examining my luggage. I awoke and saw him tugging at one of my cases. Immediately I called out to him."

"And did he answer?" The golden eyes were now without mirth.

"No. He looked around and moved toward the door. I jumped from bed . . . "

"That was so brave," Miss Jessie breathed, in exactly the same tone and rhythm as she had during the first recitation.

"A true heroine."

"Don't be ugly, Aunt Agatha. I'd like to hear the rest of Linnet's story. What happened then?"

"I grabbed at him, but he flung me against the wall. I was stunned . . ." Such a flimsy word to cover the range of pain and fury contained in my ill-used frame, as well as the sickening cloud of dislocation that had temporarily distorted both sensation and memory. "When I came to myself again he was gone."

"Indeed!" snapped Miss Agatha. "A shadow of

your imagination!"

"Was your window broken open?"

"No. He must have gone out by the door."

Dougal nodded sagely and drank deeply of his tea, the golden eyes clouded with thought. "Aunt Agatha, this morning did you find any disturbances with any of the windows or doors?"

"Of course not. The house was locked just as usual."

"We've always kept everything locked," Miss Jessie told me confidingly. "Not that we fear any of our people would harm us, but the countryside is full of vagabonds and thieves who might try to help themselves to MacLellan property . . . Being one of the area's leading families does have dangers as well as responsibilities."

"Hush up, Jessie," said Miss Agatha. "Well, Dougal?"

A smile tempered his even words. "Linnet, what Aunt Jessie says is true. We have always been extra careful in locking Jura House because there are valuables—though lamentably few of them—to tempt a casual thief. The only thing I can suggest is that you think you saw a prowler, but in reality it was an unfortunate combination of your highly strung nervous state together with your injuries. You sustained a tremendous amount of emotional grief with the deaths of your mother and my brother, then that horrible incident of your fall in the lane that hurt your head, then the trial of sleeping in a strange place . . ."

"You don't believe I saw a prowler."

"I believe you *think* you saw a prowler. Dear Linnet, it's the only explanation; none of the windows are broken, and there are only the members of the family inside the house . . . and Mrs. Giles, the cook, though I do not see how anyone even in a dream state could mistake her for a man!"

Dougal was very sincere and convincing; I almost believed him. There was nothing to be gained from insisting on a story that despite personal conviction had begun to sound more and more unlikely. Doubtless Miss Agatha would have taken advantage of my hesitation to push her views of my apparent madness had not she been called away by the insistent jangling of the doorbell. She returned with a scowl deeper than any that could be caused by a legion of actual or imagined prowlers.

"Fordyce's groom," she spat, and flung an envelope at me. "It is for you."

"Fordyce!" breathed Miss Jessie in tones that would have been appropriate to announce the Prince of Darkness.

"I say, this is outside of enough!" Dougal smote the table with the flat of his hand. "That man is using your misfortune to insinuate his way into Jura House. Linnet, I cannot urge you strongly enough to have nothing further to do with him."

Ignoring three staring pairs of eyes with what I hoped was dignified calm, I read the note, expecting, despite my family-in-law's fears, nothing more than a message of polite interest. I found something that, if they were to read it, would no doubt provoke an unprecedented storm.

My dear Mrs. MacLellan—

I trust this note finds you in improving health and happily disposed with your late husband's family. If, as I fear, it does not, please remember my offer of asylum and assistance. I shall be by if you need me.

Simon Fordyce

"It is nothing," I murmured. "He merely asks after my health most kindly." Dissembling was surprisingly easy, as long as I kept my gaze firmly riveted to the tablecloth. Miss Agatha's greed to see the note was palpable, as was her disappointment when I slid it safely up my sleeve and inwardly vowed to tear it into tiny bits at the first opportunity.

It was midmorning before my chance came. Taking advantage of the fine weather, which Miss Jessie said was sure not to last, I walked beyond the overgrown garden with a sense of freedom I had not known since running away from my mother in the park at the age of six. The oppressive atmosphere of Jura House fell away like an outgrown shell, the stink of poverty and irrationality replaced with the earthy autumnal odors of woods and fields. Beneath my feet spread a carpet of fallen leaves seemingly undisturbed for generations; ahead of me spread the edge of a glade thinning to a vista of rolling fields.

Deliberately I tore Mr. Fordyce's note into pieces so small they could be torn no further, then, feeling not a little foolish, buried the resultant mess as far beneath the leaf mould as my fingers would reach. Feeling oddly relieved, I stood and dusted my fingers as clean as I was able. Stooping to such a melodramatic action was good for me in a way, for it showed the abnormality of the atmosphere at Jura House. Here I could think clearly, as I had not been able to do since fleeing London in a fog of grief days before.

Obviously staying at Jura House was beyond serious consideration. Had my face been better healed I think I would have departed the following morning. No matter if my entire fortune were just a few pounds; even starvation was preferable to staying in the hostile atmosphere and bitter charity of the MacLellan family. Oh, Duncan, Duncan . . .

"Good morning, Mrs. MacLellan."

He was taller than I had remembered. His lips curved gently, but the smile did not reach the questioning blue pools of his eyes. He seemed to materialize out of the forest itself, and it was entirely understandable that I attributed the sudden rush of alien feelings coursing through me to surprise.

"Good morning, Mr. Fordyce."

"How do you find things at Jura House? Is it as you expected?" With an easy motion he tied his horse and leaned against the tree, looking at me with a light in his eyes that I found highly disconcerting. No man, not even my husband, had ever looked at me in such a frankly appraising way.

"No," he continued, with only the slightest of pauses. "I can hardly expect you to answer that. Shall I tell you what you've found? Two dotty maiden aunts obsessed with former glories and family pride, a brother-in-law with delusions of becoming an eighteenth-century squire, all jammed together in a sty of a farmhouse that hasn't been cleaned since they took possession. The food is shameful and scanty, and they think I am either the biggest crook in Christendom or an emissary of Old Scratch himself. Am I right? Don't worry, you don't have to answer. Your blush does it most charmingly."

"You seem to know a great deal about my late husband's household," I said, clutching desperately at the last rags of dignity.

His smile was enigmatic. "I have my ways. How is your face? Is it still painful?" With a negligent finger he lightly brushed my cheek, causing a tingling sensation totally out of proportion to his touch.

Bedazzled, I spoke without thinking. "It wasn't, until it got knocked about last night. Now it aches abominably."

"They struck you?" He glowered with an expression so fierce that my in-laws' portrait of him as an archfiend seemed highly appropriate.

"No, they didn't do anything, it's just ..." I floundered, cursing my careless tongue. I had decided to keep silent about my mysterious nocturnal visitor, but under Simon Fordyce's keen probing the entire story came out, more disjointed and peculiar sounding than before. Even to my own ears it resembled the babblings of a helpless hysteric, but he at least paid me the compliment of listening seriously.

"A prowler . . . Such things are not unheard of, I must admit, but rare in this neighborhood. You seem to bring trouble with you, Mrs. MacLellan!"

"I!"

"You." Shadowed blue eyes stared completely through me. 'Two such melodramatic incidents within two days. You have enlivened our poor country no end. What kind of enemies do you have that would pursue you to such a remote location?"

With as much dignity as possible I stood and pulled my shawl tighter. In the last few weeks I had suffered a great deal, all from events out of my control. It is my firm wish to be strong in my chosen faith and bear with Christian fortitude the trials heaped upon me, but such a resolve did not mean having to listen to gratuitous abuse from a relative stranger!

"How dare you! I have never heard such insolence!"

"Or such honesty?" Quickly he gripped the hand I had raised to strike him, rendering it useless for such a purpose, but a quick spark of surprise flashed over his face. "No, you don't, my girl!"

"I am not your girl!" I hissed, too far gone in anger to be able to do more than hurl barbed retorts more suitable to a nursery squabble. I have always envied the characters in books who had the facility to frame lucid and cutting arguments during a heated quarrel, to excel in statesmanship even during the heights of furious passion. Unfortunately, I turn either inarticulate or lamentably florid.

Incredibly, he smiled as one would at a spitting kitten or pouting child. "So you do have fire beneath that well-mannered primness! Who would have thought it? Did Duncan MacLellan ever see you like this, with your eyes glowing?" His voice was low, almost whispered, but with a strange, excited energy that both alarmed and stimulated me.

"Release me this minute!"

"Not until I tell you something . . ."

With a maneuver that spoke more of physical prowess than ladylike manners, I wrested my arm free of his grasp and took a step backwards. "I am not interested in anything you could say, Mr. Fordyce."

He glowered; the dark brows knit into a line across his forehead, from underneath which his eyes shot bright sparks. It would appear that he was not often crossed or challenged. "Someday it would be a pleasure to change your mind, my girl, but right now you shall both hear and heed me whether you wish or not. Leave Jura House. Leave Kilayrnock. Go back to London, or wherever your people are. You must get away from here."

I have never responded well to ultimatums. "You should be writing melodramas for the music-hall stage. They are quite popular now."

"Listen to me. You must leave now. Your safety depends on it!"

He would have taken hold of me again, but I moved backwards and placed the barrier of a fallen tree between us. Had the footing underneath not been so slippery and unsure I probably would have bolted, which would have been the worst thing possible. To show fear to an animal or a madman only increases their mania and your danger, and at the moment Simon Fordyce certainly did look—well, perhaps not mad, but certainly furiously angry.

Despite queerly unsteady knees, I held my position, trying to take the greatest advantage of my unfeminine height. "It is no business of yours what I do or where I go, Mr. Fordyce. Kindly remember that!" My unruly tongue ran on of its own volition. "Do you think if I had anywhere else to go in the world I would have come here? Your interest in my actions goes beyond that of propriety, sir," I added with belated hauteur, ashamed to have been caught in such rampant emotionalism.

He did not try to stop me or speak to me again, though I walked away in the sure certainty of being shouted at or having hands laid on me again at every step. When I at last gathered enough courage to look behind me, the woods were empty.

It was a difficult hour for me. I stayed in the woods, trying unsuccessfully to pray and then, when my fervent supplication to the Lord for guidance produced no tangible answers, tried to apply a course of rational thought with equally barren results.

No one wanted me in Kilayrnock; everyone was most vocal about their desire for me to go. Had I in some unwitting fashion caused the incidents of my attack on the road and the prowler in my room, or was I indeed mentally afflicted, as Miss Agatha had been so quick to suggest? Or were they just too niggardly to feed me—poor as the food was? I was accustomed to poverty, though not to being the object of an antipathy that bordered on hatred.

That was another thing I found odd; Duncan had never pretended to be wealthy, but from his conversation about his home and the few plans he had shared with me about the future of the MacLellan family, I had received the definite impression that they were at least fairly well-to-do. After all, people who speak, however casually, of investments and heritages do not usually live in dirty hovels.

At the end of an hour I rose, chilled and unsatisfied. The weather had turned with the suddenness of which Duncan and Miss Jessie had spoken, going from vibrant blue and gold to gelid grey, embellished with a cold wind and a thin moistness that foretold rain to come. The woods were no longer beautiful, but somehow sinister with darkening shadows, so much so that I hurried back and was most unabashedly running when I reached the ruined garden of Jura House.

Dougal was waiting for me, all but wringing his

hands and with an oddly excited light in his eyes. He crossed the terrace and grasped my shoulders, pulling my light shawl closer about my neck.

"Linnet! Where have you been? You must be chilled to the bone! We have all been worried to death about you. I said it wouldn't be like you to keep us waiting like this . . ."

"Waiting? I don't understand . . ."

"I'll say I forgot to tell you," he said, with a smile so like Duncan's that my heart turned over painfully. "Though it really is bad of you to disappear like that and make us give courtesy to that damned Simon Fordyce for this long."

"Simon Fordyce! Dougal, please tell me what is going on!"

The golden eyes clouded with confusion. "Mr. Cameron. Our solicitor. He said he wished to see you today. Sent a note that he would be here this afternoon, though I must admit I was shocked that he should have had the temerity to request Fordyce's presence too."

"Why didn't you tell me he was expected? I should not have gone walking if I had known that your solicitor wished to see me!" I snapped, then felt a quiver of unease at the splay of disbelief over my brother-in-law's face.

"But Linnet. I did . . . No matter. Come in." He would say nothing more, but hustled me through the long window into the stuffy darkness of the parlor.

At best, the smoke-begrimed parlor of Jura

House was a funereal tomb of shabby old furniture; when lit inadequately by poor candles and filled with a disparate assortment of people all staring at me with emotions ranging from curiosity to hostility, the effect was indescribable. Miss Jessie was agog, eyeing the drama about her with greedy pleasure; Miss Agatha was still and disapproving, with icy eyes for both me and the equally unwelcome Mr. Fordyce. As for that worthy gentleman, he looked surprisingly comfortable, but his glance at me was one of speculative curiosity that made me very uneasy. As for the important Mr. Cameron, he proved to be a rotund little man with the face of a currant bun, a pompous way of speaking, and a totally inaccurate picture of his own consequence.

"Come, Linnet, you're all wet with the mist. Sit here by the fire. You must learn not to wander the woods. We don't want you becoming ill," Dougal said with a tender solicitude totally out of proportion to my condition.

"I do hope you realize what a stir you've caused, Linnet," Miss Agatha hissed, her words as sharp as tacks.

"If I had known my presence would be required I should not have gone out," I returned evenly, and was alarmed by the indefinable look that passed between the members of my family-in-law. "It is a pleasure to meet you, Mr. Cameron. Mr. Fordyce . . ."

Mr. Cameron harrumphed and rattled the papers he held. "Now that you have at last decided to return, Mrs. MacLellan, I shall attend to business. It is not my practice to be so precipitate about the disposition of a will, but business of a lengthy nature calls me to Edinburgh and your late husband was most demanding about the terms of his last testament being known as quickly as possible."

"I must admit I find this all puzzling, Mr. Cameron," Dougal said easily, seating himself on the fender by my feet and effectively knocking off most of the meager heat the hearth produced. "Duncan's will is important, of course, but hardly so immediate. Everyone knows the terms of my brother's will. He and I both wrote such documents on attaining our majority."

"And they most certainly do not call for the presence of this . . . this interloper," Miss Agatha added with a killing glance at a sublimely unaffected Mr. Fordyce. "I cannot see where he is required regarding any business of the MacLellan family."

Such open rudeness left me gaping, but none of my other companions seemed to notice. The interloper gave her a warm smile which—probably intentionally—made her flush more deeply with fury.

"Believe me, Miss MacLellan, I have no idea of why my presence was requested, but I had enough respect for Duncan MacLellan to respond to one of his last wishes gracefully."

Miss Agatha spluttered her way into a black silence. I would have sworn that the ghost of a smile played over Miss Jessie's pale lips.

"Liar," Dougal breathed. Mr. Cameron

continued sorting his papers, while Dougal stared so intently it appeared he was trying to read them from the back.

After a measurable amount of time, Mr. Cameron at last deigned to break the unnatural quiet. "I regret to contradict you, Mr. MacLellan, but Mr. Fordyce is here at the late Mr. Duncan MacLellan's request." Disregarding my relatives-in-laws' collective gasps of disbelief, Mr. Cameron at last found the paper he wished and calmly continued. "The late Mr. MacLellan made a new will at the time of his marriage, as is entirely proper with an estate of this magnitude, and he sent me a copy."

There was another gasp in which I joined, but it was Dougal's twisted face and snarled ejaculation that grasped the solicitor's attention. "A new will!"

"Indeed. I find such haste highly unusual, but the document was most properly prepared by a respectable firm in London and is entirely legal."

"What does it say?" Miss Agatha asked. I thought she would have said more, but an abrupt gesture from Dougal silenced her.

"It doesn't make any difference what it says. We'll of course contest it and get the old will reinstated." Dougal snapped with surprising venom, but Mr. Cameron continued on in his measured way.

"That would not be advisable, Mr. MacLellan. It is most explicit and most simple."

Mr. Cameron," I murmured, "I don't understand. Duncan did not tell me about making a will . . ."

His expression showed surprise. "You knew nothing of this? Extraordinary!"

Simon Fordyce spoke, his rumbling tones somehow alien to the dark little room. "Perhaps you should tell them all the terms of the will, Cameron."

"And what do you have to do with this?" Miss Agatha stabbed at him.

"By the express request of the late Mr. MacLellan, Mr. Fordyce and I are the executors of the estate," Mr. Cameron announced sonorously, ignoring the general exclamations of shocked disbelief.

Only I was silent, having no idea of what to say.

"I have the document here for all of you to read, but it basically states that aside from bequests to Miss Agatha and Miss Jessie MacLellan to ensure a comfortable maintenance for the rest of their lives, and the deeding of Hillside Farm to Mr. Dougal MacLellan so that he can follow his dream of farming, the entire estate, under the guidance of Mr. Fordyce and myself, is to devolve wholly and completely to Mrs. Linnet Hudson MacLellan, widow of the deceased. I don't have the final figures here, due to my hurried departure, Mrs. MacLellan, but I believe with the cash lodged in the late Mr. MacLellan's bank in Edinburgh – which is not a great amount – and the values of the properties included you should count on being heiress to at least twenty-five thousand pounds."

Chapter 6

Twenty-five thousand pounds. Twenty-five *thousand* pounds! The figure ran through my head like a heartbeat. Twenty-five thousand pounds!

No wonder then that Duncan had talked so casually of his investments and bonds. Despite the squalor and parsimony of Jura House, the MacLellans were exceedingly rich—at least to the tune of twenty-five thousand pounds.

And Duncan had left it all to me, the daughter of a manuscript copyist who seldom in her life had twenty-five pence to call her own. I could barely conceive of that much money. All my life had been spent haggling over pennies and watching every ha'penny, each so laboriously earned and with so many absolutely necessary places for it to go.

I remembered my dear mother turning the linen collar and cuffs on her one decent dress again and again so as to scrape a little more wear out of it. I remembered the cold rooms and in the bitterest days of winter staying in bed all day because there was nothing to spare for a fire. I remembered the long hours of painstaking work under poor and sputtering candles to earn a small bounty for early delivery.

Now I was heiress to twenty-five thousand pounds; how much pleasure only a small fraction of that would have brought my mother. It was sadly ironic to think that now I was in a position to repay her a little for all her love and care just after she had passed on to a Region where she was receiving well-deserved rewards far greater than any available here on Earth.

Oh, Duncan! my soul cried. *How wonderful you were to provide so magnificently for me, but why should it have been ordained that you should leave me when I needed you so?*

The prospect of possessing such a magnificent fortune was less pleasant when coupled with the fact that I was alone. Sometimes to combat my loneliness I retreated into a fantasy of what life at Jura House might have been had Duncan lived; I painted Miss Agatha as a stern but just historian of the family, Miss Jessie still as sweet but less in her sister's imposing shadow, and Dougal as his brother's loving support and right hand. My dreams even extended to a rejuvenated Jura House, sparkling with fresh whitewash and smelling of soap and beeswax.

Small as it was, at least that part of my dreams could come true. If an unkind Fate had decreed that I should be denied the pleasure of making a home for my beloved husband, at least I should have the privilege of making his home a proper monument to his memory.

I determined on this some days after Mr. Cameron's astonishing announcement, days that were remarkable mainly for their loneliness. By making me an heiress, Duncan had also made me a pariah; the two aunts avoided me as if I had some communicable disease, leaving rooms when I entered them and dining in their sitting room. I feared Miss Jessie was too simple to understand the ramifications of the situation, and doubtless would have treated me with the same vague kindness had she not been so under the domination of her unrelenting sister. Miss Agatha treated me in no way at all, obviously hoping that if ignored I would disappear.

Dougal made no secret of the fact that he disapproved of the situation, but at least he had the courtesy to realize that it was none of my doing. I could not trust my friendship with him yet—the beloved familiar features with the alien being inside them were still too much for my lacerated heart to bear—but his was the only company afforded me. During those lonely days he occasionally joined me for a frugal supper, though at luncheon he was usually in the fields.

When he was with me in the gloomy dining room, our food was served in silence, but during his absence I was treated to a running growl of complaints from Mrs. Giles. The first appearance of this creature had almost been enough to convince me of supernatural apparitions; aged and filthy, she seemed to have been with the house since it was first built centuries before. Greasy locks of no-color hair straggled from under a limp and filthy cap that was only slightly less dirty than her dress and apron, neither of which she ever seemed to change. At first it was only her unpleasant odor that convinced me that she was not a spectral revenant from some earlier, less fastidious century.

"Twarn't no foolishness about serving meals in two places afore ye came," she would mutter, slinging a plate of greyish meat and unrecognizable vegetable down before me. I have taken the liberty of putting her words into a free translation, for she spoke in such a thick accent that it was some time before I ascertained that she was speaking English instead of some strange Scots dialect.

"Aforetimes there warn't no complaints about plain food nor plain living . . ."

It was the same litany she recited every meal, but that day, the afternoon of my decision, I suddenly could bear it no longer. I had been in a storm of emotions all day, dying of loneliness and hurt by the fact that when I had knocked at the aunts' sitting room Miss Agatha had closed the door in my face and refused to reopen it.

I had only been driven to the extremity of disturbing them in their lair by the oddity of finding my Bible—my mother's confirmation Bible, and the only book I owned—gone when I had looked for it in search of spiritual consolation. It had been on the table beside my bed, and now was nowhere to be found. All this, coupled with the almost unbearable itching of my wounded cheek, made the old servant woman's insolence the proverbial last straw.

"Mrs. Giles!"

She did not even bother to turn around. "Aye?"

"First of all, you will face me when I speak to you," I raged, ignobly taking my anger out on this helpless target. "I will hear no more of your impertinence. You will cook decent meals, you will serve them in a civilized fashion, and you will address me as Mrs. MacLellan, or you will be replaced!"

One rheumy eye peered at me through a straggle of hair. "Aye, ain't ye a fine lady, giving orders just as if ye was gentry. The mistress has said what ye were and how ye entangled poor Master Duncan into marrying the likes of ye . . ."

I watched in wordless fury as she hobbled off to the dark regions of the kitchen. Doubtless the old besom was soft in the head with age, but Miss Agatha could not use feeblemindedness as an excuse; I had no doubt as to whom Mrs. Giles had meant by "the mistress," and even less about the type of foulness she had told of me.

I wonder if even in such extremities of temper I should have involved Simon Fordyce in my wild plans had he not happened to come along at that particular time. Certainly I was in bad enough odor with the hostile strangers who were my family, and not even bringing their worst enemy into what was essentially a private matter could make the situation any worse, but my dear mother had raised me both by example and by rule to act on one's own recognizance and take the consequences accordingly. She had married against parental wishes, but, her father having been proved right, would not slink back to her family asking that the mess she had made be straightened out for her. No, she had gone ahead, lived her life, and raised me as best she could with help from no one. For this strength of character I admired her greatly, though I did wonder at the character of her father, who could cast out a child of his body and forget her as if she had never been.

There was no servant to answer the door, so when the bell tolled I went myself. It was the first time the bell had rung since the day Mr. Cameron had come.

"Good afternoon, Mrs. MacLellan."

The bulk of Simon Fordyce filled the doorway. The sun was behind him and he appeared as a black hulk, tall and faceless and imposing. It could have been alarming, but at the moment I was so hungry for companionship that even Old Scratch himself would have been welcome if he could carry on a sensible conversation.

"Mr. Fordyce! What a pleasant surprise. Won't you come in?"

He stepped into the cramped entryway, a smaller figure following along behind him as if caught in a wake. "With pleasure. I met Dr. Monroe on the high road and decided to tag along for a visit."

I extended my hand, grateful that Mr. Fordyce had given me such a clue. I could not have remembered what the man who had treated me that dark and dreadful night had looked like. "Dr. Monroe. It's such a pleasure to meet you formally at last."

He was a round little man with a soft voice and soft hands. "It is my pleasure, Mrs. MacLellan. At our last meeting you were not really at your best."

I opened the parlor door. "Won't you both please come in and sit down?"

What a difference in my life that simple act made. In showing those two gentlemen into that musty, dark parlor with its shabby furniture and gloomy paintings I was conscious of an emotion I had never felt before: that of possession. For the first time in my life I was receiving two visitors in a place that was mine; I wanted it to be pretty and be able to serve them tea and the type of delicacies of which I had only read. Perhaps it was the bad taste left in my mind by Miss Agatha's calumny, but I wanted to prove myself a lady.

I fussed around, apologizing for the lack of refreshments and opening the muffling drapes; that was a mistake, for it showed the dust encrusted on every surface, but to draw them again would only compound the error. Luckily the doctor was an understanding man who saw more of the human heart than the human environment, for he waved his hand negligently.

"Please don't worry, Mrs. MacLellan. I cannot stay long. I only wanted to see about your stitches. If you would just sit here in the light . . . ?"

I sat docilely in the chair he indicated and turned my injured cheek to the strong light from the west window, all the while conscious of Simon Fordyce's unsmiling gaze. It was a direct scrutiny, too unvarnished to be considered polite, and for the recipient somewhat unsettling.

The doctor's fingers were gentle against my cheek. "Have you been having any pain?"

"No . . . it's been sore, of course, but no real pain. The itching has been about to drive me mad, though . . ."

"That's good, that's good," he purred; then, at my affronted look of surprise added, "itching usually means that the wound is healing cleanly. As far as I can tell, this is just about as good as it could possibly be. Now if you'll sit very still I'll take those stitches out for you."

'Take them out?" I asked in a thready voice. It had been bad enough having them put in when I had been half-conscious; to sit calmly in the parlor while he took them out . . .

"Did you think I would just leave them in? I'm proud of my skill with a needle, Mrs. MacLellan, but I should hardly think that you would want to go around the rest of your life with my handiwork in your cheek!"

Dr. Monroe chuckled as if he had made a joke while rummaging in his little black bag.

"Taking them out is much less painful than putting them in, Mrs. MacLellan," Mr. Fordyce said gently. His eyes had never left my face. I wished he wouldn't stare so; it was rude as well as unnerving. "I don't think you'll feel much of anything."

Dr. Monroe paused. "Perhaps you would feel better if some of your family was here. Could we send for Miss Agatha, perhaps . . . ?"

My lips drew into a tight line at the thought of the spectacle of Miss Agatha being sent to comfort me, especially when she found her archenemy comfortably ensconced in the parlor.

"I don't think that would be a good idea, Monroe," Mr. Fordyce said easily.

"What? Oh, of course not, of course not. I had forgotten. I'm sorry, Mrs. MacLellan."

So the whole neighborhood knew our business! I had often heard of the lack of privacy in rural areas, and in the anonymity of my London life had thought such closeness appealing; now I felt vulnerable and somewhat exposed, as if I had been caught doing something that was not quite proper.

"Think pleasant thoughts," said Dr. Monroe, "and it won't hurt a bit."

He was almost right. I stretched my courage to the utmost and grabbed the chair arms in a grip of grim death, but beyond a very bearable prickling and tingling felt almost nothing. My eyes I kept firmly closed; the sensations were easy to bear, but the sight of those snipped black threads would be more than I could countenance. In the time-honored way of physicians, Dr. Monroe oohed and aahed, touching my cheek and muttering wordlessly to himself.

"That's about it, Mrs. MacLellan. Just keep it clean and it will be right as rain. There'll be some redness and swelling for some weeks yet, but I think after a while you'll barely be able to see where it was, if at all."

"That's wonderful news," I breathed, not knowing until that minute how much I had worried about having an hideously marred face. Even when cleaning my teeth I had scrupulously averted my gaze from the reflection in the washstand mirror. One look at the angry red puffiness threaded with black stitches had been more than enough. "Now if you'll just tell me what your fee is, Dr. Monroe . . ."

He hesitated and threw a quick glance at Mr. Fordyce, who continued to sit as calmly as before. "But I thought . . . The bill has been taken care of, Mrs. MacLellan."

I whirled on my silent guest. "By you?"

"Yes."

"There was no need for that. I am perfectly capable . . ."

He waved a negligent hand. "You forget that I am executor of your late husband's estate; paying bills is one of my functions."

Well, I was not sure whether it was or not,

especially on a matter that was so intimately personal, but it sounded reasonable, and I had an idea that any argument with Simon Fordyce was doomed to be lost. The man gave off an aura of raw power and inescapable will that was both annoying and slightly frightening. Even now, in a house full of people who happily wished him dead, he sat easily in a faded and uncomfortable overstuffed chair as if he owned the place.

"Then I thank you," I murmured. It was difficult to know what to say next. Normally I am neither shy nor tongue-tied, but had it not been for the doctor humming happily to himself while he repacked his bag we might have sat there forever in silence, as if enchanted.

"I'll be leaving you then, Mrs. MacLellan. I doubt you'll have any trouble with your cheek, but don't hesitate to send for me if you need me. My surgery is on the village high street."

"Thank you so much for coming, doctor . . ." Like puppets in a marionette show we went through the rituals of parting, I for one all too conscious of Simon Fordyce's unwinking gaze. He made no move to leave, and when I joined him after showing Dr. Monroe to the door, he had not stirred.

"Well, Mrs. MacLellan! Now how do you like your inheritance?"

If I had taken my time about answering I should have thought of something polite and noncommittal instead of blurting out what was in my mind, which had apparently been growing there since the first day I knew this was mine.

"Not at all in its present state, if you really want to know. I cannot imagine Duncan living happily in such squalor."

"Is it any easier to imagine your husband crossing the wishes of Miss Agatha?"

My back stiffened at his lazy question. "I do not like your inference, Mr. Fordyce."

"I intended no insult to Duncan's memory, Mrs. MacLellan. We had only begun to know each other before his last trip, but I was impressed with his desire to do the best he could for this valley. Apparently he spent most of his youth in school and only came here for holidays."

"Saint Andrew's," I forced through numb lips. "Near Fife."

During the relatively few times we had not been engaged in the private and nonsensical ritual murmurings of love, Duncan had spoken of the disciplines of his school and the humiliations endured by the younger boys. It had been made bearable only by the expanding horizon of learning spread before him. Duncan had said that Dougal had merged into the social life of the school like a fish taking to a broad ocean, but that he himself had found solace and companionship only in books, an attitude thought highly proper in the heir. Looking back I could see that he had mentioned his home very seldom; I hadn't thought of it at the time, for my eyes and mind had been full of his eyes and his voice, and the feeling of his lips on mine.

"Yes," said Simon Fordyce, his saturnine face a careful blank. "All the sons of the local gentry go there. He hadn't been down but a year or two, I believe . . . I wish I'd had a chance to know him better."

So do I, my heart cried. My lips said, "Where does one procure servants?"

If he saw the rim of moisture in my eyes he made no sign, nor did he seem surprised at my abrupt change of subject. "Servants? I haven't the vaguest idea. I'm sure Mrs. Wright would know. Are you wanting to engage some?"

"I have no choice. There is only a half-mad old woman who does the cooking, such as it is. I've tried, but . . ." It was true; I had tried, but the state of Jura House was beyond the efforts of one person. Only a full-scale assault by many hands would make Jura House livable. "I did the housekeeping for Mother and myself, but we never had more than two rooms, and none of them were ever as bad as this!"

His lips curled slightly at my indignation. "I can believe that. So . . . What do you want?"

"A new cook," I replied promptly. "I suppose we'll have to make some provision for that poor old creature; I don't know how long she's been with the family, but she's in no state to care for herself, and I doubt if anyone else would hire her."

He nodded. "As executor, that falls in my province. I'm sure Cameron would agree to anything I do in that area. What else?"

"A couple of good strong girls for scrubbing . . . everything in this house needs scrubbing!" I
added with feeling. "Also, I'd like one maid. Someone to
answer the door and keep things neat after we get it
cleaned up. Is that extravagant?"

He chuckled. "Hardly. A house of this size
would normally take three or four full-time servants."

"Three or four! Good Heavens! Once it's clean
I'm sure one girl and I can keep it that way, and if we
have a decent cook in the kitchen . . . Will the estate
extend to that? And the scrubbing girls until it is
clean?"

I had never before heard Simon Fordyce laugh.
It was a rich, rolling sound that boomed in the dead
and dusty air of the parlor. "Lord love you, yes, girl!
You don't really comprehend yet that you are quite a
well-to-do young woman, do you? I thought by now
you would be ordering new clothes . . . there is a
dressmaker in the village who they say is competent,
though you will probably want to order yours from
London or Edinburgh."

His tone gave me pause; it was almost a
challenge, but a challenge to what?

"I don't understand what you mean. Where
would I wear new clothes here? I have one good dress
for church, and as for anything else . . . I am still in
mourning. Everyone seems to think that because I
lived in London my life there was very social . . . it
wasn't, but I can't seem to convince anyone of that."

"You've convinced me," he said simply, and

gave me a warm smile. "When do you want your staff?"

"It's impossible, but I wish they could be here in the morning. Just as soon as you can manage will be fine."

"Once you decide to move, you don't waste time, do you, Mrs. MacLellan? Well, I'll speak to Mrs. Wright and see what can be done. In the meantime, please remember that my offer still stands."

I did not pretend to misunderstand him. "This is my home now, Mr. Fordyce."

Gracefully he took his leave, and I watched him ride away on the huge, dark horse that seemed a good match for his master. I had never had, nor even really longed for, the fancy clothes he seemed to think I should be accumulating, but somehow it did seem a shame that the first time I received visitors in my husband's home I should be wearing a dress twice turned and clumsily dyed black for mourning.

Chapter 7

Obviously nothing was impossible where Simon Fordyce was concerned, for the next morning, just as I sat down alone to an inedible breakfast, the doorbell rang. To have callers on two consecutive days, let alone so early in the morning, was an occasion, but when the callers proved to be an almost exact duplicate of Mrs. Wright who called herself Mrs. Docherty and three strapping, red-cheeked young women attired for hard work, I was overjoyed.

I was not naive enough to think that the others in the house would share my happiness, if for no other reason than that I was pleased. At any rate, I was glad to see the no-nonsense appearance of Mrs. Docherty and her three daughters, Minnie, Flora, and Lois. But I cannot say that they were pleased with anything about Jura House.

Mrs. Docherty picked up the plate on which Mrs. Giles had dumped a pod of rubbery oatmeal, sniffed it disdainfully, and put it down as if she could not get her fingers free of it quickly enough.

"And this is the kind of muck they've been

serving ye? Faith, 'tis a wonder ye still be among the living. Not fit for the pigs to eat, and if that plate's been washed in a fortnight I'll be surprised!" Her expression was eloquent. "'Tis not a moment too soon, we are. Me sister said ye were a lady sure enough, though what ye be doing in this place is beyond me."

The spate of words was almost overwhelming. The three girls nodded silently; it was apparently all they ever got to do.

I picked out one idea and clung to it. "Mrs. Wright is your sister?"

"Aye, that she is, and I'll be telling ye that nothing could have brought me into this nest o' vipers except that Maudie asked me to, though why she could concern herself with anyone from Jura House, with the exception of yer dear dead husband—nor why ye should either, ma'am, beggin' yet pardon—after the downright unchristian way they've behaved. Is this the way to the kitchen?"

I nodded, more than slightly overwhelmed.

During my short tenure at Jura House I had never ventured into the kitchen—a wise decision. Later it proved to be a pleasing room, well proportioned and cozy, but on that bright autumn morning it looked like something from a nightmare. The floor was awash with rubbish, as was the table. Cabinet doors hung open at crazy angles, food and waste stood side by side, and everything was covered in a thick scum of grease. In the sizable fireplace a small blaze flickered; Mrs. Giles crouched before it, stirring some noxious mess in the hanging kettle. The stench was overpowering.

"Lord preserve us!" Mrs. Docherty breathed. "Surely the Devil himself would be right at home in this place! What shall we be doing, Mrs. MacLellan?"

Helplessly I looked around the great dark cavern. Never had I seen such squalor. "Clean it up! We'll start here and clean up the entire house. Do you agree?"

Mrs. Docherty's deep-set eyes glowed with a crusader's fervor. "Aye, I'd like that fine! Dirt is the Devil's work!"

Her daughters nodded.

Like a little grey rat Mrs. Giles pattered forward. "What be ye doing in here? The mistress don't allow anyone to come in me kitchen! The kitchen be mine. Get out, get out!"

"The time has come for you to retire, Mrs. Giles." I was handling it badly; it was cruel to spring it so quickly on the poor deficient creature, but there was no other way it could have been done. Her look was one of pure hatred. "Please don't worry about your future . . . I have already spoken to Mr. Fordyce about getting a pension on you . . ."

"Him! Well, we'll just see what the mistress says. I'll no have ye messing about in me kitchen. Mistress'll send ye packing, see if she don't . . ." Still muttering, she scuttled away.

"Daft," 'Mrs. Docherty said succinctly. Her daughters nodded. "And now if ye'll be excusing us, ma'am, we'll be setting about it."

"But I'm going to help you," I blurted, eager to have something to do at last and someone to do it with. "I'm used to work. I kept house for my mother until she died. Besides, the more of us working the sooner it will be done and this becomes a normal house."

Mrs. Docherty regarded me intently, and for a moment I thought her opinion of me as a lady was gone, but at last she nodded. "Aye, ye'll do. Ye'll ken I've nae love for the MacLellans, but ye'll do."

It was as close to a benediction as I've ever received. As if some magical protection had been extended over me, the girls all smiled shyly, and I felt more acceptance from them than from any of my relatives-in-law.

"Minnie, build up that fire. Flora, see if the slattern has any soap about. Lois, start carting out that rubbish. If ye're going to work, Mrs. MacLellan, ye'd better be changing out of that pretty dress."

My gown was old, as all of mine were save one, but compared to the rough wear of the Dochertys, it did appear fine. I ran upstairs, feeling almost light-hearted for the first time in so very long. Now I could truly see the reality of Jura House as it might be, with the broad plank floors holystoned and polished, the plaster clean and shining with fresh whitewash.

Quickly I changed into my oldest dress. It was of flowered muslin cut in a style some ten years gone and had belonged to my mother before her body had become too shrunken to fill it. The fit was a bit tight, but it should do for heavy work. The chances that I should wear it for anything else had been so slight that we hadn't even bothered to dye it black when Mrs. Morrison and I had converted the rest of my scanty wardrobe into mourning. Even so, it felt strange to be out of blacks; the frivolous pattern of nosegays and ribbands seemed to be so far removed from the reality of my life that it might have come from another world entirely.

The stairwell acted as a speaking tube, bringing the sound of angry voices up in a wave. Mrs. Giles had wasted no time in running to Miss Agatha, who awaited me in the kitchen with wrath flaming in her face. The Dochertys stood where they were with a dogged stolidity that was heartening. I felt that I should have need of their support.

"Well, miss, just what is the meaning of this extraordinary invasion?"

Feeling as David must have when faced with Goliath—armed with right, and not much else—I endeavored to speak calmly. In size Miss Agatha was smaller than I, but her anger made her seem to fill the room.

"I apologize for not telling you earlier, Miss Agatha, but as I have not had the pleasure of your company . . ."

"Don't be impertinent! What is this?"

"Something that should have been done long ago. I am going to clean up this entire house and make it suitable for human habitation. You may choose to live in filth and eat vile food, but I do not."

Her face contorted with anger. "How dare you! Do you realize how much this frivolity of yours will cost? We must save every penny and not waste any on a temporary residence. You are taking money away from the Castle!"

A temporary residence? I thought in awe. How long had they lived here?

"Even a temporary residence can be decent to live in, Miss Agatha, and I don't think that the small amount we will spend on cleaning this place up will make much difference regarding the Castle, even if it were for sale!"

"He's a thief and a robber," she all but screamed, "and in all decency he must be forced to return to us what is ours!"

"Aggie, dear," Miss Jessie ventured timidly, the bravest of us all to approach her sister while in such a spectacular display of wrath. "It isn't good for you to get so upset . . ."

"Shut up, Jessie, and do try not to be so much of a fool. This upstart comes in and thinks just because she tricked an innocent boy into marriage she can change the way the MacLellans have lived . . ."

My impetuous tongue did me in again. "Look at this place! How can the MacLellans be proud of this, even for a night? I was wrong to do this without telling you, I know, but it all happened so quickly. We only discussed getting help yesterday and I didn't know Mr.

Fordyce could . . ."

That was another mistake. Miss Jessie's face went deathly white as if I had uttered some blasphemous obscenity, while Miss Agatha's became a positively frightening purplish red.

"He? He put you up to this and planted these spies in my own home? How dare you bring anyone like that here?"

Mrs. Docherty stepped forward, words of battle bubbling on her lips. I knew that once those two were joined, any chance of peace ever settling in this house was gone forever.

'Just a moment, Mrs. Docherty. Miss Agatha, I beg you to reconsider your words. Mr. Fordyce has been most helpful . . ."

"Shut your mouth, hussy! Do you realize how long he has tried to infiltrate people here to spy on us, to report to him what our plans are for regaining what is rightly ours? He will not rest until every MacLellan is wiped out of this valley, for then and only then will he be safe in keeping what he has stolen."

It was only then that I realized that—on this one subject, at least—Miss Agatha was not quite sane. It was not until later that I learned what I know now, and had I known it then, much needless suffering could have been eliminated, but at the moment I saw only a wild-eyed woman who seemed well on her way to becoming a Bedlamite.

"Miss Agatha . . ."

"Traitor! He gives you honeyed words and you

betray us! He's a man, and he knows you're no better than you should be . . ."

To this day I regret my next action, for I slapped the old woman across the cheek, and the sound of flesh on flesh lingered in the silent room even after I began to speak again.

"You are behaving irrationally, Miss Agatha. According to my husband's wishes, this house is now mine. I must give it the best stewardship I know how in order to make the MacLellans a good home."

Her voice had dropped to a reedy rasp. "The Castle is the MacLellan home! Have we not saved and done without for the last twenty years to get it back, only to have it stolen by an outsider who uses you as he will? Curse the day Duncan ever brought the likes of you into a decent family!"

The personal insults rolled past unheeded as the larger issue hit me like a blow.

"Twenty years! The Castle has been lost for twenty years?"

"Aye! Twenty years we've worked to get it back, and now you . . . you . . ." She could say no more. The angry eyes misted and Miss Jessie, for once the stronger of the pair, led her sister away. The sound of her hollow sobbing in the hallway tore at me.

"They've lived like this for twenty years," I murmured to no one in particular. Twenty years spent on an obsession of dead pride; what a waste! To think of what could have been accomplished for the family, for the entire valley, with the money and energy expended to recover a pile of bricks and mortar. Twenty years before Agatha and Jessie would have been young women, though perhaps past the first bloom of youth; their lives had been wasted, withered, sacrificed, in the pursuit of the Castle's recovery. I could have cried.

"Here, ma'am," Mrs. Docherty said, taking my arms and suiting her actions to her words. "Ye just sit down right here. She's a proper devil, that one. Ye be as white as a ghost and shaking too, I'll warrant. Just rest there a minute and dinna fash yersel'. A cup of tea is what ye need, no mistake. Ye, woman! Be there any tea about?" She pronounced it "tay."

Abandoned without directions by her mistress, Mrs. Giles huddled by the fire. Her face was set. "Me mistress don't allow no strangers in me kitchen. Ye'd best be getting out now. This is me kitchen and nobody else's. Cooked for the family forty year, I have, and I don't allow nobody in me kitchen!"

Forty years, I thought with awe. How had the family survived on forty years of such food—or was it that her inability to cook decently had come on only with age and infirmity? Either way, I must do my duty. Her face was full of hate.

"Please, Mrs. Giles . . . I am mistress here now. I think it would be best if you went to your room and rested for a while. Please don't worry . . . I'll do everything I can to see that you are well provided for. You've looked after the family for many years, and now you must rest."

For a moment I didn't think she would move, but at last she stood, her old joints snapping audibly, and shuffled away.

"Poor daft creature," Mrs. Docherty said softly. "She's long past any sort of work. But ye . . ." this to her girls ". . . sure aren't! Minnie, tend that fire. Lois, have ye found any tea yet?"

Whoever characterized the Scots as a dour and taciturn race never met Mrs. Docherty. Words flowed from her in a veritable torrent, directed at all and sundry, and as likely as not to herself as well. She would not let me rise until I had drunk a strong cup of tea— the first decent cup I had had since coming to Jura House—and then I was assigned the lightest of jobs.

"For yer obviously a lady born and ye shouldn't be doing this kind of mucky work," she grumbled. I assured her that even ladies learned how to work when they had to, and set about my task.

It was my lot to remove the dishes from the cupboards. Bravely I plunged my hands into the cobweb-draped shelves and tried not to think of the meals I had eaten from this same china. Lois made good use of broom and shovel, denuding the floor of its blanket of rubbish, while Minnie stoked the fire and boiled water. She seemed to be the most delicate of the trio, having a less sturdy body and a withered leg. Flora and her mother attacked the walls and ceilings with rag-wrapped sticks, dislodging generations of spiders and cobwebs.

Grime and neglect even of such magnitude

could not long withstand such an assault, and by the time we stopped to prepare a bite of luncheon the kitchen already looked more like a working room and less like a rubbish heap.

I thought Duncan would have been pleased.

Chapter 8

Gradually I got my way, and surprisingly enough Dougal became my champion. I never knew what arguments he used with Miss Agatha, but he induced her and Miss Jessie to begin taking their meals *en famille* once more, and that dreadful day of conflict was never mentioned again.

To be truthful, I had been dreading Dougal's reaction to my plans. Though I no longer mistook him for Duncan, still the thought of arguing with him was painful. Even with his own personality, he nonetheless had my beloved husband's face.

I still remember the trepidation with which I heard his returning footsteps that day. Mrs. Docherty and her girls had gone home with promises to return early in the morning, having extracted my pledge to do nothing more with the dishes than carry them into the kitchen, a stipulation on which I had insisted despite Mrs. Docherty's notion of what a lady should do. Dirty dishes left overnight on the table spoke to me of slovenliness.

Mrs. Docherty had cooked a delicious dinner of potato soup and fresh bread; peasant fare, perhaps, but it was better and more wholesome than anything I had yet tasted in Jura House. At my directions, trays had been carried to the aunts' sitting room and to the still-sulking Mrs. Giles—that night I was too tired to deal with any more scenes—and I was sitting in lonely splendor in the grim dining room when a dusty Dougal entered. He was tired and stained from his labors in the earth; while he washed up I brought his dinner from the chimney oven where it had been holding warm for him.

My plan was successful; the taste of the food did more to convince him than any of the eloquent arguments I had prepared. As succinctly as possible I told him of my intentions and of Miss Agatha's reaction, though I did try to soften her part as much as possible.

He cut another slice of bread. "Linnet, my brother thought it right that you should control this household as you see fit. I cannot go against his wishes." He grinned impishly and for a moment he was Duncan, alight with good humor. "Besides, as long as you can get food like this on the table you can paint the house red for all I care. I won't tell you I'm happy that you hired servants with such strong connections to Fordyce. The man is not to be trusted, Linnet. Aunt Agatha is a bit dotty when it comes to the Castle and the family, I'll admit, but she is right about one thing. Fordyce will not rest until he has this valley under his control, and the only way he can do that is to eliminate the MacLellans."

"Oh, Dougal, I'm sure you exaggerate . . ."

"Perhaps a little, but not much." He extended his hand to cover mine. "Maybe this is a good thing, for while they are carrying information about us to Fordyce we can be extracting information of our own. Just be cautious in what you say, Linnet."

"I cannot believe him such a villain."

Softly his eyes bored into mine. "That is what he wants you to think. Listen to me, Linnet! My property is safe; it is mine and he cannot touch it. It is for you to be worried, for you and for your inheritance."

Oddly enough, his concern was more convincing than any of his learned arguments. I was well aware that whatever physical attractions I possessed were not in themselves sufficient to interest a man of the world like Simon Fordyce, and neither was a man like that easily moved to charity.

"I appreciate your concern, Dougal, and I will try to do what is best for my husband's family."

"I know you will," he said with assurance. "What do you plan to do regarding the rest of the house?"

"Clean it! Scrub it until it shines! Polish the floors and put fresh whitewash on the plaster. And clear out this room. This table's much too big and that painting is enough to give me indigestion!"

He laughed and choked on his soup. "Carry on, oh fair crusader! I've always hated the thing myself."

"I'd like to see the house bright and clean," I

said dreamily. "I know Miss Agatha is upset with me for taking money away from the estate instead of saving it for the Castle, but I always wanted a home of my own . . . someplace pretty . . ."The yearning in my voice revealed rather more than I had intended to say.

Dougal shrugged. "Don't worry about that, Linnet. What you spend renovating this place won't make that much difference either way, and this will make a nice dower house or manager's residence when we recover the Castle."

"Do you think Fordyce will sell?"

"He'll be forced to. He cannot be allowed to keep what is the traditional property of the MacLellans." He spoke with a calm determination that was somehow more chilling than florid oratory. Apparently none of the MacLellans were rational when it came to the subject of the Castle.

"Oh, I meant to ask you, Dougal . . . Have you seen my Bible about?"

"Your Bible?"

"Yes, my mother's confirmation Bible. It's brown and about so big . . . I can't seem to find it. I was wondering if perhaps you had seen it?"

Dougal shook his golden head slowly. "No, I don't remember anything like that. I'm sure it will turn up. That reminds me of something, though. Wait here."

He was back some minutes later, a pen and inkwell clutched in one hand and a huge book cradled in the crook of his arm. With a flourish he placed them in front of me.

"The family Bible. We should have had this little ceremony long ago, but it's been so long since there has been a bride in the MacLellan family, I didn't think of it until this moment. I suppose our mother was the last."

With deft fingers he riffled through the thick pages, opening the book to where in a variety of inks and handwritings the history of the MacLellan family for the last hundred and fifty years was inscribed. Almost with a will of their own my eyes raked down the list, barely taking in the Anguses and Moiras, the Charleses and Faiths, until they reached the present. There were Agatha and Jessie, only a few years older than their brother James, who had been married to an Alice and had died on the same day as she, some two weeks after the birth of their twin sons.

Postponing the inevitable pain, I looked up questioningly at Dougal.

"Our mother was never very strong. She was a Southron—an Englishwoman—and too weak to endure life up here. She lost three children before Duncan and I were born and having us killed her, though she lingered for two weeks afterwards. I don't think Aunt Agatha ever forgave her for dying."

I felt a wave of pity for the weak, unknown Alice. There was a bond between us, two English wives in a strange and hostile land. I was certain that Miss Agatha had disliked her too.

"And your father?"

"He killed himself when our mother died. He couldn't face life without her." Dougal's voice was flat.

"But the babies . . . you and . . . Duncan. Didn't he realize that you needed him?"

His eyes were empty mirrors. "You are so naive, Linnet. Aunt Agatha used the same argument. Our father said he wanted nothing to do with the murderers of his wife."

"But that's horrible!"

"He was maddened by his grief." Dougal shrugged. "Perhaps if he could have been restrained . . . He got away from Aunt Agatha though, and flung himself from the Castle battlement. My grandfather was alive then, and with the dominie's help got my father buried in consecrated ground, but he was never the same afterwards. It was only a year or so later that he lost the Castle and we were reduced to living here."

My gaze went back to the Book. There he was, Charles Edward MacLellan; he had died the year they had come to Jura House. I felt a fleeting flash of sympathy for Miss Agatha. It had not been an enviable position; her only brother dead by his own hand, her father dead after losing the family seat in a wager, left with two infants and a weak-minded sister in her care. Now for the first time I could see how she had become as bitter and cold as she was.

And the next set of names . . .

Two baby boys born on the same day, one name with a painfully recent death date already inscribed beside it. Dougal must have put it in the Book as soon as I had notified him. For a moment the inked characters blurred and swam as my eyes filled with tears. Dougal placed the pen staff in my numb fingers.

"Sign."

"Sign? Shouldn't you do it? You're head of the family now." A wave of emotion strong and fleeting as a flash of lightning passed over Dougal's face. "I'm not used to hearing myself called that, Linnet. I never expected to be. No . . . You must sign. It's traditional."

With trembling strokes I penned my name and date of birth opposite Duncan's, immortalizing us forever as man and wife, even if for so brief a time. Linnet Hudson MacLellan. My writing looked shaky and strange, so very different from the polished copperplate in which I had copied so many manuscripts.

"There," said Dougal with a smile. "That's done."

* * * * *

The house began to pull together much faster than I had expected. Mrs. Docherty and her girls were miracle workers who regarded dirt as a personal enemy and untidiness as a sign of moral degeneration. They scrubbed and scoured the kitchen until everything in it shone, then moved on like an industrious army to the rest of the ground floor. Rugs were mercilessly beaten, releasing clouds of dust undisturbed for years. Walls were washed free of soot encrustation and whitewashed. The drapes were beaten and hung out to air while the good weather held.

Room by room the cleaning progressed, leaving behind a different house in its path, as if the real Jura House were just waking from a long slumber. At my insistence, Dougal had hired a young crofter to do the heavy lifting and make repairs as we found them necessary. He was kept quite busy, as it appeared nothing had been done to the place in years. Perhaps it was because there was so much to do, or perhaps because he found Flora Docherty's shy smile intriguing, but Willie Campbell all but moved into Jura House.

For a while it seemed that perhaps my dream of a home with a family was really going to come true. Under Dougal's influence both aunts had been persuaded to come out of their sitting room and, in body at least, rejoin the family. Miss Jessie was plainly overjoyed at the restoration of the house, seeing a happy future of tea parties and afternoon callers. Miss Agatha of course did not share her sister's raptures, seeing in each scrubbing brush and bar of soap that much more money stolen from the Castle, but she did not mention the subject, and life took on a pleasant, even tenor until I committed some new stupidity.

One of these was when I asked about church. During the first few days of my time at Jura House I had been too dazed with grief to think of anything else, and then I had thought that the others had refrained from suggesting it out of respect to my disfigurement. Now that the stitches were out and the washstand mirror confirmed that there was only a slight discoloration left, I began to feel the lack of Divine Services. Until the extremities of her last illness, Mother had insisted that we attend worship at least once a week.

"Church!" Miss Agatha's eyebrows soared upward as if I had suggested something immoral.

We were sitting in the newly refurbished dining room. The parlor was still in a state of flux, with furniture stacked every which-way and the plaster scrubbed clean but not yet whitewashed. I was justly proud of the dining room. The offensive picture had been removed to the attic where it awaited some unknown disposition. After we discovered that the table possessed an ingenious arrangement by which parts of it could be removed without affecting the function, it had been reduced to a workable size. Now there was room for Flora to carry the food around for service, and one no longer felt it necessary to shout in order to carry on a conversation with someone sitting on the other side of the table. So far I had hung no decoration to replace the unlamented painting and the pristine plaster walls, broken only by the heavy, dark beams, were pleasingly rustic.

"Yes," I answered all unknowing. "I presume there is a House of Worship in the village?"

"Oh, yes." That was Miss Jessie. Her voice was soft: and breathless as a girl's. "I can remember dear Papa saying that it was a fine example of Norman architecture. Some parts of it date back to just after the Conquest, you know. It has the prettiest glass windows . . . Papa gave the biggest one as a memorial to our dear Mama. There are lots of memorials there, for it seems that people just keep on dying, no matter what, but most of them are just silly old plaques on the wall. They aren't pretty like Mama's window . . ." Miss Jessie was just as bad as Mrs. Docherty when she got going.

"Oh, do hush up babbling, Jessie," said Miss Agatha without heat, working at her needlepoint. She stabbed at the canvas viciously.

"I was just answering Linnet's question, Aggie. During the summer the church society holds a bazaar and at Christmas there is a big party . . ."

"Jessie!"

"Oh, I know you think such goings on are disrespectful when connected with a church . . ."

"The Lord doesn't need all that social flummery. Two good sermons a Sunday and a God-fearing congregation of decent folk are all that's needed."

That should have warned me, but a day of exhausting physical labor and a moment of relative peace on top of a substantial meal had dulled my wits. Dougal had separated himself from us and was sitting at the opposite end of the still-sizable table lost in some weighty tome about progressive farming methods.

"Perhaps," Miss Jessie said wistfully, "but the socials were fun and I do miss seeing everyone . . ."

"We do not need their kind."

"Don't you go to church?" I asked incredulously.

Miss Agatha's eyes impaled me with a cold glance. "We do not!"

"But why? I should think that worship . . ."

"We worship the Lord as was intended, with simplicity and decency. We do not need to go into a church where those who profess to be honest people receive interlopers and thieves!" Miss Agatha gave an offended sniff that nearly echoed off the walls. "He even has the temerity to occupy the laird's pew."

"And of course we do not want to run the risk of meeting that horrible man socially!" Miss Jessie twittered as if she expected him to materialize out of the shadows at any minute. There was no doubt as to whom either of them meant. "We've managed never to speak to him until he brought you here. Of course, you couldn't help that, Linnet dear, but . . ."

"She could have sent word that she was coming instead of being so foolhardy as to try and walk from the station at night." Miss Agatha's tone was venomous.

"I did send word, Miss Agatha," I replied wearily. "I wired before I left London."

"I remember one year the Duke of Cumberland

came to visit Papa for the shooting. Mama was still alive then, and all the ladies of the church came to tea . . ." Miss Jessie's tone was painfully wistful. "I remember the house was so full of people, and there were comings and goings all the time . . ."

Later Miss Jessie's remark was the only reason I could think of for dreaming about heavy footsteps going quickly through the house that night.

Chapter 9

All the good that had been gained was lost when Simon Fordyce came to take me for a drive. The unseasonably warm weather had held longer than anyone had thought it would, and we were taking full advantage of the fact to air the smell of soap and whitewash from the house. Miss Agatha and Miss Jessie had haughtily declined to help in the cleaning; in their eyes no lady did that sort of manual labor, but they knew better than to comment on my participation. Dougal was gone nearly all day, overseeing my property as well as his own, and came home at night so exhausted he could scarcely eat.

I was on my knees in the newly whitewashed parlor, energetically applying wax to a table leg, when the doorbell rang, and moments later a smiling Lois announced Mr. Simon Fordyce. He strode in, looking about the place with the unconscious arrogance of an inspecting buyer; I remembered Dougal's warnings about this man, but could not find it within myself to resist his raw power and magnetism. Clothes have never been important to me, but it was surely a great shame that on our last two meetings I had looked so shabby.

"Good afternoon, Mr. Fordyce."

His eyes raked the room, and he smiled. "You've done wonders with this place. I didn't think it could look so good."

"That's a fine compliment indeed, sir. Won't you sit down ? Please forgive my not offering you my hand, but at the moment I am all over wax."

He sat in the chair I indicated, one whose newly brushed upholstery and gleaming wood attested to my industry. "Are you not satisfied with the Dochertys?"

"Most certainly. They are excellent workers. Why did you ask?"

"Surely it is not usual for the lady of the house to work like a navvy alongside her servants."

Somehow his words irritated me, as if work were something not quite respectable. How chagrined Miss Agatha would be to know that Mr. Fordyce and she actually agreed on something! I stood, shaking my skirts free of dust in order to obtain time in which to marshal my thoughts. It wouldn't do to offend Mr. Fordyce, not when he had been so kind to me, but neither could I forget that I was now a MacLellan, and according to my brother-in-law, this man was a sworn enemy of our house.

"I have never been used to idleness, sir," I said carefully. "There is nothing onerous about hard work when it is for the good of one's family. I could not be more pleased with Mrs. Docherty and her daughters, but many hands finish the job more quickly."

A wide smile split his face and his blue eyes so filled with warmth that for a moment I felt as if I were melting. "Well said, Mrs. MacLellan! You sound like a true lady of the old school instead of one of these modern misses raised to be nothing more than a useless ornament. Duncan MacLellan showed rare sense in marrying a woman like you."

Luckily he went right on talking, for I could have said nothing. A scalding blush rose and fell, flooding my face with tingling pinpoints of heat. Compliments have not been so numerous in my lifetime that I could handle them easily.

"It's a shame to waste this weather indoors, Mrs. MacLellan. It won't hold much longer, and the gloomy days seem to last forever. I'll wager you haven't been out of the house since you came. Go put on a pretty frock and I'll show you some of the countryside. You really should see it before winter settles down in earnest. I'll wait right here."

It never occurred to me to question him. I rose and all but ran upstairs. At least I didn't have to dither over what to wear. My only decent dress was the one Duncan had bought me, the one in which I had been married, the one in which Simon Fordyce had found me sprawled in the road that night. I washed and changed quickly, brushing my untidy hair back into the simplest of chignons, pausing only to seize a clean handkerchief.

Except that my handkerchief box was empty. I owned only a few nice handkerchiefs and kept them carefully folded away from the unadorned cotton squares I used for everyday, but I looked through the plain ones just to make sure they hadn't somehow been misplaced. Like most people with few possessions I am careful with them and not prone to mislaying them, but after the incident of my mother's Bible I could take no chances.

Yes, I had found the Bible. It appeared under my bed where I would have sworn I had fruitlessly searched several times. After quizzing each member of the household so often on its whereabouts to no avail to have to report that it had been found under my bed was humiliating. Miss Jessie and Dougal had been almost patronizingly kind, saying that it would be difficult to see a dark brown book in the shadows under a bed, but Miss Agatha had been more abrupt, hinting that I had caused the problem deliberately to draw attention to myself.

It was no use. I searched through all my scanty possessions that barely filled two drawers of the big old dresser, but there was no trace of any handkerchiefs save the plain cotton ones. It was distressing, for I distinctly remembered putting them there when I had unpacked. I did not see how they could have been misplaced in another drawer. These two had been hurriedly cleared out for me, their contents jammed into the other drawers, which still held the things of Duncan's he had left here before leaving for London. I had never had the courage to open them.

And I still didn't. Telling myself that Simon

Fordyce was waiting and I didn't want to keep him, I took a plain hanky, slammed the drawer shut, and scampered out as if my problems would stay there.

"Linnet, I should like to talk to you a moment." She stood across the passageway like a barrier.

"Could it not wait, Miss Agatha? I have a visitor."

She sniffed, managing to fill that simple sound with a multitude of meanings, none of them flattering. "I am aware of that, as well as of who it is. What do you think you are doing?"

"Mr. Fordyce has offered to take me for a ride around the countryside ." My cloak was over my arm and the one decent bonnet I owned dangled from its strings around my wrist. There would be nothing to be gained by dissimulation even if I weren't certain that she knew everything.

"And you are willing to shame this family by going, you traitorous hussy? Have you no respect for your husband's memory?"

Luckily for everyone involved, Miss Jessie chose that moment to stick her head out the door. Her smile never seemed to change, nor did her bobbing curls.

"Why, Linnet, you're all dressed up! Doesn't she look pretty, Aggie?"

"Thank you, Miss Jessie," I said as evenly as possible. "Excuse me, Miss Agatha. I shall be back before long." I swept past her, feeling her hot eyes boring into my back.

Simon Fordyce was waiting by the window. He turned away from the uninspiring view of the garden and smiled without mirth.

"I'm sorry I have kept you so long."

"It wasn't long at all," he replied mechanically. He took my cloak and draped it over my shoulders, then waited patiently while I tied my bonnet strings with shaking fingers. It had been a mild enough confrontation with Miss Agatha, even including her personal attack on my character; what I was dreading was the scene that would ensue after I returned.

Mr. Fordyce handed me gently into the carriage. "I'm sorry. I had hoped . . . I didn't mean to cause you any unpleasantness."

"You heard?"

The carriage creaked and tipped as he crawled into the seat beside me. He draped a lightweight carriage robe over our knees as protection against the chill autumn air, then clicked to the horse. As we rolled out along the disgraceful drive, I could literally feel Miss Agatha's disapproval flooding out after us.

"I couldn't really not hear. The stairwell from the hall carries sound extremely well."

"I hope you will forgive Miss Agatha . . ."

"My dear Mrs. MacLellan, anything Miss Agatha MacLellan could possibly say to wound me has been said many times over by now, and has long since lost its sting. My main concern is any distress she might cause you."

Oh, how nice it would be to relax and pour into his sympathetic ear all my worries and ask his opinion about all the incompatibilities and contradictions of my new family, but Miss Agatha's bitter words prevented me. According to them, this man was the sworn enemy of our family, yet Duncan had chosen Simon Fordyce over his own brother to administer to the estate. My head swam.

"I cannot really blame her for disliking me, sir. From her point of view I am an interloper. If Duncan had lived . . ."My voice faded.

"If Duncan had lived," he repeated in a very different tone; then, "We shall talk of your husband later, ma'am. For now, let us concentrate on the scenery."

It was easy to do. Once we had left the depressing aspect of the Jura House drive, the countryside wove its spell of peace. I did not really notice in which direction Mr. Fordyce drove; instead, my attention was captured by the shifting subtle colors of the landscape. The horizon was a smudge of smoky blue at the far corner of the world. Between there and the prosaic stone walls that lined the road lay a palette of muted browns and greys and golds, their colors blurred as if they had melted and run together. The individual fields were defined by a webwork of stone fences that cut across the colors and snaked their way over the hills.

Even the air had a different feel to it, thicker and more sparkling than in London. The light breeze that whipped our faces was chilly but clear; it did not yet carry the sullen coarseness of winter. Different odors—some of which I recognized and some of which I did not—played and intermingled through the air almost like music. There was the strong dark influence of the brown-scented earth and the homely smell of animals; over this were the lighter notes of some late-blooming flower, sweet and pungent, and a queer sort of tang that could have been the scent of the sky itself. To one reared on the stench of close streets and coal fires and too many ill-washed people packed into too small a space, this was almost as heady as wine. I had never smelled anything so heavenly, and said so.

"Wait until the spring comes," Simon Fordyce said dreamily. He had stopped the carriage at the brow of a hill and the valley lay spread before us like some sort of exotic carpet. "When the snow melts and the burns start to run again after winter's ice, the whole country seems new-washed and clean. Then the growing starts and the whole air smells of green and newness. After that the flowers bloom and the heather dyes the very air itself."

My heart lifted and turned over. Anyone who could be so touched by the beauty of these hills could never be as bad as my relatives-in-law painted him.

"I never dreamed there was any place so full of such beauty. Duncan tried to tell me, but it's not the same as seeing it."

He clicked to the horse and we began to move again, down into the real world once more. "And what else did Duncan MacLellan tell you? Did he describe life here?"

"We had such a short time together . . ." Maddeningly my blush flowed upward, fueled by memory of the beloved but nonsensical conversations we had shared. "Actually, we spoke very little of anything practical. I suppose we thought we had the rest of our lives to discuss things as they were."

"Young, in love, just married . . . I cannot say I blame him," Fordyce said evenly. "Yet I cannot but wonder if he could have had some presentiment of his unfortunate end. Surely it would have been more practical to wait until he returned home and have his family solicitor alter his will in your favor."

I searched the granite profile, strongly outlined against the cloud-clotted sky, seeking any accusation inherent in those casual words. Miss Agatha had made several such comments, accusing me of urging Duncan to name me as his beneficiary; somehow it had not occurred to me that Simon Fordyce could have such unflattering thoughts, and I was oddly disappointed despite his carefully bland countenance.

"I don't know why he did it, Mr. Fordyce. I knew nothing about it until Mr. Cameron read the will. Don't you think that if I had I would have said something? I wish I had known, so I'd have had something to tell . . ." My voice had risen to a shrill peak. I sat back silent, wishing that just for once I could control myself.

"Miss Agatha?" He finished. "Yes, I can

imagine she has made your life pretty miserable about that, if nothing else. I don't know what Duncan MacLellan was thinking of, letting you come here unwarned about what you'd find ..." He stopped abruptly and smiled slowly. It was a warm smile that transfigured his face, giving it a softer, more vulnerable look. "No, I can't blame him. I was beginning to know your husband, Mrs. MacLellan, and he was no coward. If I were young and in love and married to a beautiful girl, I should do my best to protect her from the harsher realities of life as long as I could. I'd want to protect her too, every way possible."

His look upon me was as soft as any Duncan had ever bestowed, but my reaction was entirely different. With Duncan I had felt protected, snuggled safely from the cold; Duncan had exuded a gentleness that had enveloped and comforted me, whereas this man ... Simon Fordyce was a power as strong as any of those in nature, a whirlwind of energy and strength that would buffet anyone foolish enough to venture too close. I had never known a man like him; my experience with men had been mainly with the gentle men of letters for whom Mother and I worked and, of course, my own sweet Duncan.

"I'm truly sorry this comes to me, Mrs. MacLellan, but it must be done, and as executor of your husband's estate I am the one to do it." His face had hardened so that I felt a moment of alarm. "Look one more time on the beauty of this valley, for then we must look at its ugliness."

Chapter 10

Indeed, that was the most curious day of my life. After looking at the beautiful vistas created by nature, it was almost torture to descend to the man-made horrors that lurked under those pastel colors and behind those picturesque hills.

It didn't all come at once, though; first we stopped by a powerful river surging through a rock channel some twenty feet wide. Gently Simon Fordyce lifted me down from the carriage, once more handling my not inconsequential bulk with ease.

"Best allow me to take your arm," he said, leading me to the edge of the chasm. For a moment, shadowy suspicions formed mainly by Miss Agatha's convictions that he meant us all harm made me hesitate, but at the brink, on discovering that I possessed no head for heights, I was extremely glad of his strong grip. Some ten feet below, the river swirled busily beneath a cap of white foam.

I forced my stiff lips to move. "It is indeed a most powerful sight, Mr. Fordyce, but I cannot really call it an ugliness."

"It isn't. This is the Cardoc River, and perhaps the only salvation this valley has."

I didn't understand him and said so, adding, "Is the valley short of water?"

His laughter was harsh, distorting his face so that for a moment it looked almost demonic. Behind him the clouds had begun to coalesce into an opaque, angry mass. "No, my dear Mrs. MacLellan, water is about the only thing of which this valley is not short! Come along; distasteful as it might be, we must begin your education."

He did not speak again until we were a good way down the road. The short burst of bitter mirth seemed to have drained all pleasantness from his chiseled face, leaving it cold and merciless. His voice, however, was gentle.

"This is not going to be pretty, Mrs. MacLellan. Poverty . . ."

"I do not understand the reason for your concern, Mr. Fordyce. I have lived with poverty all my life. Manuscript copyists do not live a life of luxury."

Charitably he said nothing, allowing me to eat my words in silence. Our first stop was at a tiny farmhouse—croft, as they were called in this country. Poverty of the direst sort emanated from it like a bad smell. There was plenty of that, too, especially once we stepped past the low door into the cave like interior.

It was a dark, low-ceilinged room, thick with peat smoke. Even in its original condition, Jura House had been a palace compared to this hovel. The walls were blackened with soot, making the interior seem smaller and more closed in than ever. There wasn't much furniture, and what there was looked rude and homemade. A large dresser hugged one wall; there was a table draped with a cloth over the place settings waiting for the next meal; a battered old box bed stood next to the filthy fireplace. There was only one window, a tiny affair in the wall opposite the fireplace, hardly bigger than a peephole and hung with sacking.

These details I recalled only later; at first my full attention was captured by the straggly-haired slattern who was the mistress of the house. My mother and I had thought ourselves poor, but our life had been both clean and comfortable compared to this abysmal situation. A horde of big-eyed starveling children clung to her skirts, peering around their mother shyly to stare at the newcomers.

"Mrs. Bruce?" Fordyce had said when the door opened. His manner had been polite and not at all condescending; there was nothing to warrant the dark look of hatred that washed over the woman's face. I could not miss that, despite the flood of odors that flowed out the open door, forcing me to avert my face.

"Ye'd not dare come here if my man was home," she hissed and then spat, sending a shining gob of spittle onto Mr. Fordyce's boot.

Only the briefest ripple of reaction showed before his face again settled into calm lines. "I am sorry that you feel this way, Mrs. Bruce. I come on a social call. This is Mrs. Duncan MacLellan."

Her cold eyes raked me like nails. "Master Duncan's widow? I heard ye had come to Jura House. Ye shouldna be in the company of this one." Contemptuously she gestured at my companion.

"Mr. Fordyce has been most kind," I replied, more haughtily than was necessary. Surely at least the crofters could be clean!

"Since her arrival, Mrs. MacLellan has had no chance to get out and meet the local people. I thought she should learn of the valley's problems from the . . ."

"Problems!" she shrieked. Flinging the door wide, she all but pulled me inside. "Problems! I'll tell ye of problems! We be nine here, nine with naught but a spot of land that wouldn't feed a mouse, and me man out of work these past six months. Problems ye want, is it? I'll give ye a problem! What do ye do when yer babies cry with the hunger and there's naught to feed them? What do ye do when ye see two of yer own die and there's naught ye can do about it? Problems? There's problems enough in the valley for us. Go back to yer fine house, Mrs. MacLellan. Ye dinna belong here."

I all but fled in the face of such hostility. Never in my life had I met such vicious, vivid hatred. "The poor creature," I said when we were far enough down the road to be out of earshot. "I must do something for her . . . Send her some food . . ."

"Not unless you want it flung back in your face. The Scots are notorious for their pride, especially the poor ones. They don't take kindly to charity."

"But her children are hungry!"

"So you want to play Lady Bountiful. There are hungry children all over the valley, Mrs. MacLellan. Do you intend to carry baskets to all of them, waiting for them to pull their forelocks and say 'Thank'ee, me lady'?"

"You are being hateful!" I snapped, and wondered why it bothered me so. "What else can be done? Those children must be fed."

"What else, indeed?" he murmured enigmatically, flicking the horse into a trot.

All in all we visited half a dozen such homes that afternoon, with very little variation. The hostility, the poverty, the staring eyes . . .

It was late afternoon and the sky was heavily overcast with clouds like wet wool when we at last turned back towards Jura House. I was exhausted in both body and mind. The stench of such abysmal poverty as I had never before seen seemed to cling like a sticky residue, and the memory of those hungry, hateful eyes . . .

"Are you tired?" His voice was unexpectedly gentle.

"Yes, but not just physically. I had no idea that such conditions existed . . ."

"I didn't think that you would. It isn't something ladies should concern themselves with. It seems, however, that you have no choice."

"I? What do you mean?" Even as I asked, there was a growing certainty in the back of my mind, and just as strong a conviction that I did not want to know.

"This is what nobody has wanted to show you, Mrs. MacLellan. I'd try to shield you myself if it were possible, but . . . it is your responsibility. Everything we have seen today belongs to you. The people are your tenants. What do you intend to do about them?"

My thoughts of the last few minutes were confirmed, but I had no pleasure in their validation. So this was the legacy Duncan had left me; a quarrelsome family, a fair amount of money, a great deal of beautiful but apparently unproductive land, and the responsibility for God only knew how many hungry people. For a moment my head swirled from sheer fear; I could run away, resume my maiden name . . . In a city like Edinburgh or London no one would find me and point fingers, saying You are responsible . . .

Of course that cowardly phase lasted only a moment. I could not so easily slough off Duncan's trust. Obviously he had wanted me to be cared for, that was why he had made me his heiress; but had he realized the weight of responsibilities that went with it, weight that I was ill-equipped to carry?

"Why haven't I been told this earlier?"

Fordyce smiled at me with a warmth I could feel all the way across the carriage. "I knew you'd make the best of it. Plucky little thing, aren't you? As to why you haven't been told, I don't know. Cameron's still out of town, Miss Jessie probably doesn't know herself,

Miss Agatha . . . Miss Agatha probably doesn't give a damn, begging your pardon. Her sole interest is getting the Castle back."

"And Dougal? He rides the land every day."

"I cannot presume to explain Dougal's motivations for not telling you," he said primly.

"Mr. Fordyce, you are being less than honest with me. Please! Duncan chose you as one of his executors over his own brother. How am I to make any decisions at all, let alone the right ones, if I do not have sufficient information?"

"You impress me, Mrs. MacLellan." He drove on in silence for a few more minutes, then pulled the carriage over under a spreading tree. "It's not very businesslike, but the Castle is too far away and I can't see us being allowed to have a civil, unfettered conversation at Jura House."

"This is fine," I said and pulled the carriage robe higher. The breeze had picked up, soughing through the crisp leaves above us with icy breath and making them rattle like chattering teeth. "Please explain."

"I'm afraid I cannot be impartial in this; my own side . . . well, this is the basic cause of the hostility between your brother-in-law and myself."

"I gathered that."

His eyes were hooded and lazy, but I could still feel their power. "I knew you did. You remember when we stopped at the Cardoc River? Yes, that's your property too. I have been trying to buy that piece of land. It isn't very big and no good at all for farming, but the MacLellans won't part with it."

"Why on earth not? I should think as hungry as they seem for money they would jump at the chance." Perhaps that was unkind to my adopted family, but in all truth I could not see Miss Agatha turning down any sum that she could squirrel away to save against the reclamation of the Castle.

"That's what I thought, but . . . I didn't buy the Castle with an idea of setting myself up as a country squire, Mrs. MacLellan. I chose this valley for several definite reasons, not the least of which was that gorge we just saw. I could see a textile mill built there . . ."

"A textile mill!"

"Yes. The river is strong enough through that narrow gorge to provide all the power we could ever want. As you know, there is a rail connection at Kilayrnock. The area is riddled with unemployment and hunger; it should have provided a sizable work force anxious for regular jobs." His voice was unbearably wistful.

"It sounds perfect, and yet it obviously isn't. Why not?"

"I'm beginning to think young Duncan knew what he was doing when he left everything to you. I'll tell you why my dream isn't working, Mrs. MacLellan. I gained the enmity of Miss Agatha when I bought the Castle; Miss Jessie of course follows her sister's lead in everything."

Already the pain was coming, but I had to know.

"And Duncan?"

"I respected your husband, Mrs. MacLellan. Don't mistake me; we weren't friends and probably never would have been, but he was an open-minded young man who had the best interests of his people at heart. I think if he had lived he would have come over to my way of thinking."

"What was stopping him?"

"Dougal. Dougal and his aunts and that bedamned starving aristocrat pride of theirs! Please forgive me for swearing . . ."

"I've heard worse," I said with wry humor. During the summer nights in London the windows had been open, allowing the heat-born quarrels to drift upward into little waiting ears. "Please go on."

"I first came to this valley searching for a mill site, as I've told you. Mr. McPhail was an acquaintance of my father's, so it seemed normal that I should stay with him. I saw the Cardoc Gorge and knew this was the place I had been seeking. Old Mr. McPhail was getting old; he had no heirs. He wanted to sell the Castle and live in comfort in Edinburgh for the remainder of his life. I needed a place to live. It's much more than I need, but I thought it was customary in these backwater places for the people to look up to those who lived in the neighborhood big house . . . I didn't know what a mistake that was." The magnificent .shoulders shrugged in a gesture perilously close to defeat.

"Dougal said something about a debt of honor . . . That Mr. – McPhail, was it? – should have offered . . . the Castle to the MacLellans first."

"Why bother? He had been willing to sell it to the MacLellans for years, but it became more and more evident that they would never come up with a reasonable offer. The MacLellans couldn't raise a quarter of its worth."

My mouth dropped. "A quarter! You must be tremendously rich, then!"

For a moment he stared at me, then his rich, booming laugh rolled out. "Oh, my dear, dear innocent! Did you think your inheritance was all in cash?"

"I am unfamiliar with inheritances . . ." I stammered through a rising blush.

"Most of your inheritance is tied up in land, according to the papers Cameron sent me, with some in bonds and very little in cash. I doubt if the MacLellans could raise over two thousand pounds in ready money. Any more, and they would have to start liquidating, which they would never do. I had the cash, Mr. McPhail wanted to sell . . . it seemed the best at the time."

"And now?"

"Dougal MacLellan is blocking me at every move."

"Why?"

"He fancies himself as a feudal lord over this valley, or at least as an eighteenth-century squire. And such dreams do not encompass any sort of modern factories or mills, and certainly do not allow for any other authority in his fiefdom."

"I cannot see why the two could not coexist peacefully," I said slowly. "If the mill would use only a little bit of unfarmable land . . . It would guarantee an income for those poor creatures, and the land could still be worked . . ."

He looked at me keenly, his expression unreadable. "You are a woman of rare common sense."

"What was Duncan's stand?"

"Did you know your trust puts me in a very uncomfortable position? I could tell you anything I wanted to make you decide in my favor, but then you look at me with those clear innocent eyes and I can't do anything but tell the truth." He cupped my chin in his hands. "You are a very dangerous woman, my dear."

For a moment the earth stood still; then it began to wobble dangerously as if it would break apart and go spinning off into space. My blood boiled as thickly as the low-hanging clouds.

"How can the truth be dangerous?" But I already knew the answer.

"Dear innocent . . ."

Pulling my whirling senses back into a semblance of decorous restraint was one of the hardest things I had ever done. In another moment I should have abandoned all decency, led on and ever on by a pair of glowing blue eyes. With trembling hands I adjusted my bonnet, and when I again looked out from that respectable frame of black silk, Simon

Fordyce had retreated once more into nothing more than a dutiful escort.

"You were going to tell me about Duncan."

"You should have a hat, a fluffy little thing with veils and feathers. Bonnets are old-fashioned," he said quickly, then shrugged as if casting off a weight and went on in quite a businesslike tone. "Duncan MacLellan was as stiff-necked as any of them, and who can blame him? Raised by two family-mad aunts obsessed with past glories . . ."

"He disapproved of your project?"

"At first. He was also a very conscientious young man. He took his responsibilities to the valley very seriously. I like to think that he would have come to my way of thinking. The past is dead; Scotland has no need of more aristocratic squires and land-bound vassals. The future needs prosperity, Mrs. MacLellan, and true prosperity can only be created by men like me, men who start companies and create jobs. There will always be a need for farmers, but on land like this it's a losing effort. Companies and jobs are the future. Perhaps your husband had come around; after all, he did make me an executor."

"I am reminded of that continually, Mr. Fordyce, and can't help but wonder why."

He ran tense fingers through his rumpled hair. "I can't tell you why your husband chose me, Mrs. MacLellan. We had talked several times about the mill project, but when he left for London he was still not in favor of it. I'd like to think that while he was there, he changed his mind. His primary concern was the people of the valley. Maybe his naming me was a sign of approval . . ."

The grey day drooped lower, falling about us in large wet chunks. Simon Fordyce made a move to start the horse moving toward home, a gesture that was abandoned when I laid my hand on his. My lips were stiff, but not with the growing cold.

"Perhaps it was, Mr. Fordyce," I said with prim propriety, yet I could not help but wonder . . . *Of what use was such a gesture if Duncan didn't expect to die?*

Chapter 11

The cold cloth was not only soothing to my aching head, it provided a convenient close darkness wherein I could shut out the world and think. I could hear the muted sounds of the household going on downstairs, homey and familiar sounds that seemed so distant. Supper would be on the table before long, and one of the Docherty girls would be sent up to fetch me. I had until then to prepare myself for what must come.

And come it would; that I had known since I left the house this afternoon under Miss Agatha's icy disapproval, and had had it sharply reinforced not long ago when Dougal, white-lipped with anger, had materialized out of the grey misting rain in front of our carriage.

He pulled the horse to a plunging stop, forcing Mr. Fordyce to swerve sharply to avoid an almost certain collision. Both animals were nervous in the inclement weather punctuated with explosive clashes of thunder, but it was the smoldering enmity of the two men, stretching between them like a darkly glittering sword, that made me feel uncomfortable.

"Linnet, are you all right?"

"Of course I am, Dougal," I replied as evenly as possible, hoping that Mr. Fordyce would overlook the insulting aspects of that simple question.

"Thank God," he spat. "I've been searching . . ."

"That wasn't necessary, MacLellan," Simon Fordyce said in as even a tone as could be expected. "Mrs. MacLellan is quite safe in my care."

"Safe! Coming around to the house, sneaking her out from under our very noses, exposing her to God only knows what kind of heresies and keeping her out in the rain . . . It would have been so easy to find a barn or croft, wouldn't it, just to lay over the rain . . ." Dougal's face was distorted with some inner rage.

"You have a filthy mind," Fordyce returned warmly.

I do not like being cold, I do not like being wet, and I especially do not like being the focal point of two grown men making fools of themselves. I thought longingly of a fire and hot tea and, strangely enough, of the far-away sanctuary of Mrs. Morrison's cluttered little sitting room, the closest thing to a home I knew.

"Am I a prisoner then, Dougal?" I asked in sharp annoyance. "Cannot I accept the offer of a ride from a neighbor without your presence and permission?"

Dougal whirled on me, his white face showing surprise that I should speak back to him so. "Of course not, Linnet . . ."

"Then there is no problem, except that you are keeping us from going back and I am getting drenched!" I knew that such defiance would doubtless be paid for by an angry scene later, but I was indeed getting extremely wet and angrier by the minute; I was no scullery maid or companion who had to ask permission to leave.

The trip back to Jura House was short and, as I had expected, Simon Fordyce refused my obligatory invitation in for some tea.

"No, my dear Mrs. MacLellan. The Castle is not that far away and I am not so much of a weakling that a little more wetting would hurt me, but neither am I a Daniel to walk unafraid into a lions' den." His unflattering words were tempered by a singularly sweet smile, and suddenly I wished more than anything that he would come in for tea, even if it meant still more unpleasantness later.

Impatiently Dougal handed me down from the carriage and all but shoved me into the house. I was saved for a little while since one of the Docherty girls—I could not tell which, since my eyes were blurry from what I thought was the rain—made a horrified comment at my condition and whisked me upstairs for a brisk rubdown and then dry clothes. Since Jura House did not possess the amenities of a groom, Dougal would be busy for some time yet seeing to the comfort of his horse.

Flora, for so it had been, brought me a cup of steaming tea, saying that the Misses MacLellans would be having theirs in their room. Her eyes were pitying. After this last ugliness, I supposed the Dochertys would leave and Jura House would fall once more into the slovenly stasis it had known before. At that moment I was as low as I had yet been since coming to this place. Perhaps it would be best if I took a small competence for myself, signed the rest of the inheritance over to the MacLellans, and went away to build a new life for myself.

Eyes. Pale, hollow eyes of starving children, peeking around their mother's torn and dirty skirts. I could not forget them. Duncan had not only left me the land and the money, he had left me the charge of their welfare. To which MacLellan should I entrust it? Miss Agatha, all too ready to consign the rest of the world to perdition so long as she and her sister could resume what she regarded as their rightful place as owners of the Castle? Dougal, nourishing a dream of a style of living belonging to a previous century? Or even to Simon Fordyce, with his modern ideas and plans for progress?

Duncan, my heart cried, *how could you have gone and left me alone without even a hint of what you wanted me to do?*

I suppose it was then that the memory of Duncan's belongings coyly skirted the edge of my mind, and had I been undisturbed, the thought might have developed then into full flower instead of waiting to call me from sleep later that night. But just then there was a short rap on my door and a voice softly calling "Linnet?"

The reprieve was over; now I had to face them.

"Come in."

Wearily I took the cloth off my eyes and dropped it in the bowl on the bedside table. Flora had left one lamp burning; it cast a feeble gleam against the dark plaster and darker woods, which looked even dirtier than they were by comparison with the refurbished ground floor. My housecleaning fervor had not yet reached the upper floor, and the contrast was startling. Once more I was struck by the impersonality of the room. My husband had apparently had this room since early childhood, yet it bore no imprint of his personality. The furniture was shabby, but might have once been good; the plank floors were innocent of carpet, being dotted here and there with home-made rugs. The draperies and bed hangings were of a somber green and had obviously been adapted to this room from some other, grander chamber. It was a strange room, more similar to a third-choice guest room than the bedchamber of the heir.

"Don't get up, Linnet." Dougal's pale face swam in the yellow lamplight, his expression of tender concern so like Duncan's that for one mad moment I found it almost possible to pretend . . .

No! Duncan MacLellan was dead! It was against the laws of both God and man to try and seek his resurrection in his brother.

He had changed out of his dripping clothes into a long, well-worn dressing gown. His hair was still wet, however, and lay darkly plastered against his head.

"Are you well?"

"I have a slight headache."

"You must take very good care of yourself," he murmured and seated himself on the edge of the bed. "We must take no chances of you becoming ill. Grippe and influenza are common here."

"I am seldom ill," I said with as much dignity as I could manage under the circumstances. His casual seat on the bed made me very uncomfortable. Besides the doubtful propriety of it, his being there reminded me painfully of the short time Duncan and I had enjoyed the intimacies of matrimony, when before bedtime he would sit beside me in just such a way and we would murmur the sweet nonsense that was meant for ourselves alone.

"That is good." He gently smoothed a damp lock of hair back from my forehead. It was a simple enough gesture, but under the circumstances took on an aura of intimacy that was unsettling.

I knew enough of the world of my mother's girlhood to know that in London's polite society for me to share a house with my brother-in-law would be just short of scandalous, even with the twin dragons of Miss Agatha and Miss Jessie there to lend propriety as chaperones. However, this was not London; still, I found myself wishing suddenly that Dougal would take up residence at the farm Duncan had willed him and give me time to think without my senses being clogged with memory at every turning. How could I ever hope to learn to live without Duncan MacLellan when his double shared the same house with me, tantalizing but untouchable?

"You hurt me this afternoon, Linnet. Did you do it deliberately?"

I was taken aback. "I? Hurt you?"

"Yes. When you all but accused me of keeping you prisoner."

"That is how it appeared, Dougal. You rode up out of the rain, stopped our progress back here, and started making wild accusations . . ."

His smile was so like Duncan's! "Dear Linnet, are you so sure that he would have brought you back here? There is a law here in Scotland; all he would have had to do would be to seek shelter claiming that you were his wife. In Scotland, you have but to represent yourself as husband and wife to be considered married."

I struggled not to laugh at his earnestness. "Surely you are joking! First of all, he knows I am in mourning . . ." I suppressed the half-born, astonishingly seductive image of what it would be like to be married to Simon Fordyce. "Second of all, we hardly know each other."

For a moment Dougal buried his face in his hands. When he looked at me again his expression was incredibly tender. "I hardly know how to say this without sounding insulting and that I do not want to do, but think for a minute, Linnet. He talked his way into owning the Castle; he tried to get Duncan to sell him the land; now he seems intent on befriending you . . . I am afraid that he sees you not as the lovely creature that you are, but as a means to possessing the land he wants."

It was a logical argument, but my inner mind rejected it out of hand. I would not believe such a tale. One of the customers for whom mother and I had worked had been a lady novelist, much given to wild adventures, powerful villains, idiotically innocent heroines, perfect heroes, miraculous rescues, and supernatural happenings. She paid well and her books sold mightily, but they had given me an early and deep distaste for that sort of melodrama. Dougal's insinuation was far too close to one of her plots.

"I cannot accept such wild theories, Dougal." Feeling the inequity of our positions, I struggled to sit upright, my back braced against the uncomfortably carved bedstead. "Mr. Fordyce has been kindness itself." I wanted to add that he had helped me more than those who might have been expected to do so, namely Dougal and his aunts.

"Of course. It is to his benefit to do so. Duncan left you in control, Linnet, and I am without say. It pains me to see you turn so much to this man who has sworn the downfall of our family, fill the house with his creatures and place yourself helpless in his power . . ."

"You make him sound some sort of monster!"

"I'm trying to make you see him as he is!" Dougal beat his fist against the counterpane in frustration.

"Duncan himself made Simon Fordyce one of

his trustees . . ."

"And that is suspicious in itself! Linnet, Linnet, my dear . . . sister, Duncan and I were twins and twins possess a bond that is much closer than ordinary brothers. We were closer than anyone could imagine."

So close that he never even told me you were twins? my unruly mind asked, but my lips kept silent.

"Can you see what it meant to me to find out that he had written another will?" Dougal's eyes were pained. "I do not begrudge you the estate, Linnet; believe me. I do question why it was done in such a hole and corner way, and why I was not one of the executors. I find the whole thing exceedingly strange."

"You're trying to tell me something. What?"

"I am trying to make you see the connection between Duncan and Fordyce! Duncan wanted the best for his people, so when he came into his majority he tried to find the best way to help bring prosperity back to the valley. It had been sadly mismanaged during his minority and he . . . he always wanted everything in such a hurry!"

I nodded, remembering the precipitateness of our wedding; patience had not been counted among Duncan's virtues. "Are you suggesting that Mr. Fordyce had anything to do with Duncan's writing a new will? I didn't know they were that close."

"I can't prove it, but I'm sure Fordyce was behind it. Duncan had talked to him about that accursed mill, thinking perhaps it was a way to help the valley. I know he went to London to investigate further, despite all my pleadings to the contrary. When Fordyce left not long after Duncan, I became suspicious; he had said he was going to Edinburgh, so I followed him but I lost him there and spent days trying to find him again. I never did." The implied horror clung to Dougal's words and hung in the air long after their sound had died.

"You're implying that Mr. Fordyce had something to do with Duncan's death!"

"It fits, Linnet! Look at it with a mind unclouded by that man's smarmy charm!"

Smarmy was not the word I would have used to describe the bracing blast of Simon Fordyce's personality, but the rest fit. Dreadfully so.

"Fordyce follows Duncan to London and finally convinces him. In the meantime Duncan meets you, marries you, and in an excess of zeal, wanting to protect his new bride, writes a new will at Fordyce's urging naming you as heiress, with Fordyce as one of the executors."

"But," I objected, gathering in every ounce of logic, "what would be the point if Duncan had agreed?"

"Because even if Duncan agreed, he could disagree later, especially once he came back to the valley and we talked some sense into him. But if Duncan were dead and his innocent widow owner of everything . . . how much simpler just to marry the widow and gain control without opposition."

For a moment my head swam and I heartily wished myself as far away as possible from Jura House and its tangled webs, until a vagrant memory of my mother came back to me. We had been sitting in the sunlight, having moved the table over to the one window, and I had been reading from the lady novelist's tortured manuscript while Mother proofread her fair copy. It had been some nonsensical story about the prince of a mythical country, and everyone had been quick to believe the worst of him for the flimsiest of reasons—all except the loyal heroine, of course. Mother had been unable to restrain her giggles, saying that anyone silly enough to believe such a mishmash deserved to be separated from their sixpence. "We are lucky enough to be living in a country where proof is needed to adjudge guilt," she had said in a strangely serious tone of voice. "One man's word should never be enough." At the time I had thought it odd such a stupid story should have produced such a solemn reaction; it was not until years later that I learned my father's army career had been jeopardized by a single accusation. Though he had been proved innocent, the incident had begun the downward slide that pulled him and my mother a little lower each time until he disappeared from our sight forever.

"You sound as if you have been reading trashy romantical novels," I said at last. "I cannot accept such villainy in one who has shown me nothing but consideration. Please Dougal, I know you have reason to believe as you do, but I cannot see it that way. Like Duncan, like all of us, I want nothing but what is best for the people of the valley." I evaded the offer of his outstretched hand and stood.

He stood too, bringing the warmth of his body so close I thought I would suffocate. He was so like Duncan, with his shoulder just the right height for my head, his arms the right length for holding me, the slight bulk of his slender body so familiar and yet so alien . . .

With gentle hands he cupped my face, turning it upward until our eyes were but inches apart. "I am not as good nor as altruistic as you, Linnet. My main concern is for you."

Chapter 12

The gong had sounded twice for dinner, and yet I lingered, hiding in my bedroom like an animal in its den, certain that when I went downstairs the kiss that Dougal had placed so tenderly on my lips would be visible to all like some scarlet brand.

When at last I did force myself to go down, the others were waiting in their customary seats around the newly reduced table. The hostess's chair at the end of the table waited for me; long Miss Agatha's place, she had ostentatiously and bitterly given it up to me in a nasty little scene right after the will had been read. I sat there, but I never got over the feeling of a little girl playing grown-up under a disapproving adult eye.

"You're late, Linnet. I hope you were not harmed by this afternoon's wetting." Miss Agatha's tone made a lie of every word.

"I apologize," I replied, ringing the tiny silver bell to signal the beginning of dinner. It was a refinement that Mrs. Docherty had suggested, a gracious touch that saved the necessity of having a servant stand on duty in the dining room. That seemed overbearing for a simple meal *en famille*.

We waited until Flora had passed the soup plates around. Once more Mrs. Docherty had done her magic; how that woman could clean like a fiend all day and yet produce such heavenly meals three times a day was beyond my comprehension. Fordyce's creature or no, she was a jewel and I would have wept salt tears at the thought of losing her.

"You must be very careful of chills, my dear," Miss Jessie burbled, slurping her soup. She for one was pleased with the new regime in the house, bragging about the food and talking hopefully of callers and tea parties in the spring. I could imagine what Miss Agatha thought about the tea parties and callers, but no matter what she said, she liked the new menus. Already her face was less gaunt, and though she never had a kind word to say about the meals, her plate never went back to the kitchen less than shining.

"Chills can be particularly dangerous, especially at this time of year," Miss Jessie was saying. "I remember one of our aunts went out riding and was caught in just such a rain. She got soaked to the bone, and was dead in a month. It never stopped raining, either, not until after she was dead." She gave a significant glance toward the windows, where the rain, less violent now, still rolled down with wet precision.

"The weather has indeed broken," Dougal said mildly. His manner was as usual, kindly and diffident, and there was nothing to suggest the passion with which he had kissed me not many minutes before.

"Pity it did not do so yesterday," was Miss Agatha's acid comment.

I put down my soup spoon. Unless it were brought out in the open, we were all due for an unpleasant evening of sniping and innuendo; everyone there knew what the trouble was, but until Miss Agatha had unburdened her mind there would be no peace.

"And what is that remark supposed to mean?" I asked, giving her the desired entrance.

"I should think even a silly Southron like yourself should know the answer to that! Riding off with that man just as though it were a Sunday afternoon drive. The Lord only knows where you and this family would be now if Dougal hadn't ridden to rescue you!"

"Probably just as we are now, since Dougal found us on our way back to Jura House." I could not make my lips form the word "home."

"Linnet, dear innocent creature that she is, has not yet been convinced of Fordyce's desperate methods," Dougal said mildly. Miss Agatha could only harrumph.

I took my courage into both hands. "Since the subject is now in the open, let us discuss it."

Someone's spoon clattered, but I could not raise my eyes. My heart pounded so loudly it seemed that everyone could hear it.

"You have said many times that Mr. Fordyce is out to ruin us. Today he took me for a drive around the valley and showed me things that he said were mine and therefore my responsibility. We visited the crofters' huts . . ."

"The nerve of that man! Visiting our people," Miss Agatha hissed, and Miss Jessie palely imitated her. "The nerve!"

"Why? When was the last time you visited the crofters, Miss Agatha? Indeed, I don't think it was his place to show me such things, I think it was yours . . . all of you. Why wasn't I told?"

"Impertinent!" Miss Agatha spluttered, but my attention was turned toward Dougal.

He balled his napkin and dropped it to the table, all pretense of eating gone. "Why, Linnet? Because I am a gentleman and feel that a gentlewoman's sensibilities should be spared. There is nothing you can do about the state of the crofts at the moment. You have just lost both your mother and your husband. You have just given up your home in London to come here. After such emotional wrenches I thought you deserved a period of peace before showering you with the estate's problems."

It sounded so good, so kind, so much like something Duncan would say. I knew I should be appreciative, but the memory of those large, empty eyes pricked my conscience.

"I'm sorry, Dougal. I am grateful for your concern, but to consider my sensibilities when those children are starving . . ."

Miss Agatha harrumphed again. "There's always something wrong with the crofters; never are they satisfied."

"I remember when Mama and Aggie and I used to ride out with charity baskets," Miss Jessie said dreamily to no one in particular. "We'd take calf's-foot jelly and beef tea to the sickly ones, and they'd tug their forelocks as we drove past . . ."

"Shut up, Jessie. That was when they knew their place."

This bickering could go on all night. It was up to me to put the conversation straight. "I don't agree, Dougal. There must be something that can be done. Mr. Fordyce explained to me about his textile mill. What is wrong with the idea?"

Had I thrown a live snake with bared fangs in the middle of the table, their reaction could have been no more horrified. Both aunts began to expostulate angrily—on different subjects—until Dougal silenced them with one sharp word.

"Fordyce has done a good job on you, hasn't he, Linnet? I suppose we deserve that, letting him get in the first punch, as it were. I forgot that acting according to gentleman's rules can be a detriment in dealing with one who is not a gentleman."

"Not a gentleman? I don't understand . . ."

"I didn't suppose you would," Miss Agatha sniffed, putting a world of implications into those few words. "He has a flashy sort of superficial manners, but he is from trade! His father was an ironmaster and his grandfather a blacksmith!" She pronounced that as a sentence of doom.

"He came from Leith," Miss Jessie added and from her tone it was the worst imprecation of all. "He hoped to set up here as a gentleman."

Mother had often told me of how in her girlhood the social clash between trade wealth and the often cashless aristocrats had led to storms within her limited circles. The conflict had lasted only a few years, until the aristocracy had discovered that the money from trade could allow them to continue in their luxurious habits, and the moneyed trade people found that their wealth could buy them a respectability through marriage and association they could have no other way. Apparently here the difference had never been reconciled.

"I'm not interested in him," I said firmly. "I care about those hungry children in the valley. If his mill will bring prosperity and take only a few acres of land that isn't productive anyway, why don't we sell?"

"Why, Linnet? Because we don't want to see our whole way of life, the way of life of the valley for hundreds of years, disappear forever." Dougal's eyes were locked with mine. "Admittedly the mill only requires a few acres of ground, but the water . . . ! The Cardoc is the main source of water for the valley. If the mill controls the water flow, the river could be strangled. Also, he says the mill will give good employment to the men of the valley. Who's to say he'll continue to pay them after he has made them dependent on his largesse? Cutbacks in pay are not uncommon. As you see, I have looked into the matter, for I too have the valley's interests at heart."

"I don't think, . ."

"Listen, Linnet. If the mill is built, who will work the land? The fields will go fallow because the men will all be working at the mill all day. Our income comes from the farms. To build the mill would be to take the bread out of our own mouths and put it into the hands of a wealthy parvenu."

Although I am only a woman, I feel that my brain is at least the equal of most men's, and Dougal's arguments made sense. If the mill paid good salaries, of course the men would go there instead of following the riskier course of farming, leaving the MacLellans high and dry.

"And," Dougal went on, "in any society there can only be one leader. The MacLellans have been the naturally born leaders here for generations. If we allow the mill to be built, the leadership of the valley will pass to Fordyce. He doesn't care about the people here, except as fodder to feed his mill. Does he ride out to help a crofter save a mired cow, or talk to the constable when one of the men has had a drop too much of spirits?"

A memory of Simon Fordyce's gentle words when he thought I was Old Annie drunk on the road, the night I almost died but for him, surfaced and was ruthlessly pushed back down.

"Think, Linnet. Think what Duncan would have thought."

There was a long pause as I tried to do exactly

that.

"I understand," I said quietly. "The valley must come first," I added, hoping to quell the haunting memory of those pleading, hungry eyes.

"I knew you were a woman of sense, Linnet." Dougal's tone was warm and his glance all but scalded me the length of the table. To gain time I rang the little bell and Flora exchanged the soup plates for the main course. It was some sort of fish, lightly cooked and buttered. I eventually ate it all but without tasting a bit of it.

When Flora was gone I had recovered enough to return to the attack. "All right. We now have the inheritance Duncan left: me. He . . . died before he could put it to use, and that task now falls to me. What shall we do with it?"

Miss Agatha was the first to speak, her words all but stepping on my question. Animation enlivened her face and sparked her eyes, and it was possible to see a ghost of the beauty she must have had when she was young.

"Do? There's no question about that, my girl. We must get the Castle back! We must show that man he is not welcome in our valley and offer him a price he cannot refuse!"

"Aunt Agatha . . ."

"You listen to me, Dougal MacLellan! That's what we have been saving every penny for since the day our poor papa lost it. We must get the Castle back!"

Dougal's eyes flashed and he lost all

resemblance to Duncan; although, of course, I had never seen Duncan angry. "Perhaps if you had not saved every penny so ruthlessly there would be less to be done to the land now! Your damned penny-pinching starved the land, let it go to rack and ruin, and it will take damned near everything we have to make it productive again!"

"How dare you speak to me like that?" White-lipped, Miss Agatha was all but trembling with fury. "The Castle is our heritage!"

"The Castle! The Castle!" Dougal slammed his fist down on the table with a sound like thunder. "Damn the Castle! It is the land which is our heritage, the land and its people! We have had the land for untold generations, Aunt Agatha. It is not only our heritage, it is our future! It feeds us, it keeps us . . ."

Miss Jessie was making little cooing noises of distress, her bleary eyes filled with tears. I hated to see the old thing so upset, and to tell the truth, the scene was disturbing me too. Heaven only knew what the Dochertys were hearing—and, if they were Mr. Fordyce's creatures, what they would tell him.

"Please!" My voice cut across the table. "This is most unseemly."

It took a moment, but the tension dissolved. It had been almost a physical thing, filling the dining room with a tight knot of emotions, and when it vanished the air was strangely empty.

"Perhaps we should let the conversation wait until a calmer time," I began, but Miss Agatha's dictum sliced my words in half.

"There is no need. We have only one course to follow, and that is to get the Castle back!"

Dougal's temper was building up again; his eyes glittered and his mouth was tightened to an ugly line as if he were physically holding back harsh words.

"First of all, Miss Agatha," I went on as mildly as possible, "I do not think that Mr. Fordyce will sell at this time. Secondly, I know very little of such matters, but I do not think there is enough cash in the estate both to refurbish the farms and land and buy the Castle back. It would be foolish to have only the Castle and no land with which to support it . . ."

Miss Agatha's glance could have frozen water, but Dougal's approval was warm.

"Good girl, Linnet! Trust Duncan to choose not only a pretty girl but a smart one!"

"I am pleased you find her acceptable, Dougal. I for one regret the day your brother married a Southron chippie without breeding or family." The old lady's tone was poisonous.

If the emotions hadn't been so high, if she hadn't been so deliberately hurtful, I probably would have kept my mouth shut. Heaven only knows I had spent my entire life without family and never missed it, but I did have my pride, and the hateful old man might as well be good for something!

"I wouldn't say that, precisely," I returned smoothly, speaking almost without thinking. "My grandfather was a famous and much-decorated general."

Oddly enough, the reaction to that particular little bombshell came from Dougal. He started, and the color all but drained from his face. "Your grandfather? You have a grandfather? Linnet, I thought you had no family," Dougal's eyes were bitterly intense.

"It's no matter of import, Dougal. I have never met my grandfather. He and my mother quarreled before my birth and they kept separate circles ever since then." That was about as delicate a way of putting it as I could find.

"A general!" Miss Jessie breathed, her eyes shining as she doubtless visualized somehow benefiting from such a grand connection.

"I didn't mean to hide anything or keep it a secret," I babbled on, trying to break the vacuum of silence. "It just never was very important to me."

"A grandfather," Dougal muttered. Miss Agatha merely stared at me as if I didn't exist. Outside, the thunder cracked like a cannon, making us all jump.

"If you will excuse me, I must talk to Mrs. Docherty. She and her girls must not wait if the weather deteriorates any further."

No one said a word as I left.

The homey normalcy of the warm kitchen washed over me like a healing breeze. The four Dochertys sat around the kitchen table, tea mugs in hand. For a moment the scene was so cozy and domestic I felt like an outsider looking in on an intimacy that I could never share. Then someone noticed my presence, they all jumped up, and the mood was gone.

"Oh, ma'am, did ye ring and us not hear? I'm sorry . . ."

"No, Flora, I didn't ring. I'm just concerned about all of you. The weather is so bad, perhaps you'd better forget about washing up tonight and get on home before it gets worse . . . If you like, you could stay over . . ."

Four smiles beamed. "It's a true lady ye be, ma'am," Mrs. Docherty said. "Lord love ye, this ain't much of a blow. Many a time we've walked worse. Wait until ye've wintered here. Besides, I canna see Docherty getting his own dinner." At that she and the girls giggled, as if it were some sort of tremendous joke.

"Still, I'd feel better if you left now . . . it's so dark out . . ."

"Now ye listen to me, Mrs. MacLellan. We be thanking ye kindly, but a little bit of weather never stopped us from doing our jobs. We'll be washing up and going as usual. Now dinna ye worry about us and we'll be back in the morning. After all, tomorrow we starts the upstairs!" Her pudgy face glowed as if she had been promised a treat.

Chapter 13

The rain continued through the night, at last slowing to a steady and monotonous curtain of grey about the house, but Mrs. Docherty and her girls were right on time the next morning. Chattering like happy magpies, they shed their wet outer garments in the kitchen, then clattered about with mops and rags and soap and hot water for all the world like an invading army.

I had slept but not rested. The scene the night before and the chilly civility among the members of the family afterward had upset me, bringing evil dreams. By the time Mrs. Docherty and her brood had arrived and started breakfast for the aunts—Dougal by this time being far afield and I disinclined to eat in the morning—I had been up for hours.

Miss Jessie and Miss Agatha had moved their place of refuge to the downstairs sitting room, having, as Miss Agatha so succinctly put it, "no desire to be in the middle of a servants' gathering." Her implication obviously included me, but by now I was past caring. It didn't even bother me that they made such an ostentatious show of locking their sitting and bedrooms, saying that the old ways were good enough for them and they'd have none of our pawing through their things. There was still plenty to do, even though I had managed to spend most of the morning avoiding it.

I had awakened early that morning with yesterday evening's half-fleeting thought solidified. Just because Duncan had not told me anything of his wishes did not mean he hadn't made them known. It had been a habit of his to keep a diary, a sort of datebook with impressions and notes. I had teased him about how he wrote in it every night even during our honeymoon. After his death it had seemed indecent to look into it, as if I were peering into his inmost thoughts. The idea of so invading his privacy had repelled me. When I decided to come north, Mrs. Morrison doubtless had packed it, as she had the rest of his things. I had managed to pack my own possessions, but the tragic finality of touching his had been beyond me. I remembered arriving here with his case along with mine, but had no memory of them since.

I was soon convinced that they were not in my room. After dressing, I made a thorough search of the entire place. Still there was no sign of his belongings. I could picture them now; a silver-backed brush, worn with age, a plain toilet set which had seen hard use, his diary . . . They had been packed along with his clothing in an old black suitcase with tan straps. I could all but see it sitting in the corner beside my own cases on the night I had arrived.

I had a vague memory that my cases had been carried to the attic. During my perfunctory tour of the house I had been shown the attic steps, small splintery stairs leading upward from the door at the end of the hall. They were just as narrow and steep as I remembered, almost ladder-like and coming up into the centre of the shadowy cave that was the attic. Thank Heavens I had remembered to bring a lamp; the attic was windowless.

When I was young, Mother had read me a story about a young prince who found a treasure cave. The attic certainly didn't glitter with gold, but the dark shapes and tantalizing boxes reminded me of that old story. My second thought was more prosaic; this cobwebby mess would most certainly have to be cleaned.

I didn't have to search at all; my cases had been put right by the staircase as if the person delivering them had not cared to venture further into the darkness. Of Duncan's case there was no sign.

"Mrs. MacLellan? Be ye up here?" The stairs groaned under Mrs. Docherty's solidity, and in a moment her head popped up the stairwell. "Thank the Lord I finally found ye! I was beginning to think ye had been spirited away by the Old Ones! Whisht!" she exclaimed after looking around the cluttered attic. "I'd swear to glory that this place hasna been touched since the house was built." She pronounced it "hoose."

"Probably not. We need to do something

about it, but it can wait for a while."

Her laugh boomed. "Faith, it's waited long enough already! A few more days will make no difference!"

I laughed too. "I don't think so. Have you been here long?"

"Just this moment arrived. I wanted to tell ye Minnie shan't be coming today. The walking be a bit hard for her weak leg . . . the mud and all." She spoke hesitantly, as if expecting some criticism. "She hasna been strong . . ."

"I noticed her leg. Has it been that way from birth?"

"Nae, she was as hale and strong as any of me childer until she fell down the cliff at Cardoc Gorge last winter. Lay there for a night and a day, she did, her leg broke and herself knocked half senseless."

"The poor child! How did you find her?"

"'Twas yer husband, ma'am. He started hunting as soon as he heard she was missing, which is more than I can say for some as lives in the valley. He found her, then roped himself down the cliff and brought her out on his own back. Saved her life, he did, for the doctor said she couldna have stood another night in the open." Mrs. Docherty drew a deep breath like a swimmer before a dive and looked me squarely in the face as an equal. "I've worked for Mr. Fordyce and his family for most of me natural life, ma'am; along with me sister Maudie, Docherty and me came with him to this valley, and we have no love for the MacLellans. It was only because of what yer dear late husband did for me Minnie that I came here at all, and only on account of yerself that I be staying."

As if embarrassed at having said too much, she turned to go. I was touched by her rough tribute and show of loyalty, but it left the air charged with an emotionalism that would be the harder to dispel the longer it was left alone.

"Could you wait a moment please, Mrs. Docherty? I want you to know I appreciate your efforts for me and for the House of MacLellan . . ."

"For ye, ma'am, and the memory of yer man," she said with blunt honesty. "I wouldna give the time of day to the others!"

That was enough on that subject, I decided. "These were the cases I brought from London," I said, gesturing to them. "There was also a case of my late husband's things . . . it was black leather and had tan straps. Have you seen anything like that?"

"Black leather? Nae, I havena seen naught like that."

"I haven't either. I've looked for it everywhere. It's just disappeared, like my Bible did."

"A Good Book disappeared?" Mrs. Docherty peered nervously into the shadows as if expecting Old Nick himself to appear. "Faith, 'tis a sure sign the house is cursed! When not even the Word will stay . . ."

I restrained my laughter at her superstitious babble. "I don't think it is as serious as all that, Mrs.

Docherty. I found it several days later under my bed. The thing is, I know I checked under the bed at least twice. And now all my good handkerchiefs are gone."

She may have been given to the strange beliefs of those living in a wild and remote land, but Mrs. Docherty was also intelligent and a shrewd observer of human foibles. "So ye think someone's been playing tricks on ye? And using a Good Book to do it? That's blasphemy, ma'am!"

"I can't think of another explanation, save if the Devil himself did come to call, and I find that hard to accept."

Her rag-wrapped head shook slowly. "'Tis nae good to speak lightly of the Adversary, ma'am. There's a lot been going on that is only attributable to him. Poor Mr. Fordyce had his hayricks fired the night before last. Burned to the ground, they did, and him having to ship in feed from Kirkcudmathy to keep his beasts from starving, he is."

"How awful!" I cried. I had been with him yesterday and he had never mentioned it. "Do they know who did it?"

"Not a body is saying so much as a word, as if one could expect better. It's just like it was when the vegetable patch was trampled and torn up last month. I tell ye, ma'am, me sister is half-feared to go to sleep at night for worrying that she'll be burnt in her bed or . . ." here her voice dropped to a conspiratorial woman-to-woman whisper ". . . even worse!"

I had a fair idea of what she meant by "or worse," and while I found the possibility of such forced intimacy repugnant it was a great deal more appealing than being burnt in one's bed.

"This is ridiculous," I said firmly. "Such vandalism must stop! If these hooligans get away with this Heaven only knows what they'll try next, or against whom!"

"Tis proud I am to hear ye say that, ma'am. Ye being heiress to the valley, perhaps a few words in the right ears might stop things?" Taken in one way, her implication was insulting; taken in the way she meant—that as designated leader of the valley my word would be law—it was flattering. I didn't feel I lived up to either.

"I'll certainly talk to Dougal about it. We cannot have lawlessness in the valley."

"Aye, ma'am. Be ye coming down to breakfast, or did ye fix an early bite?"

"Neither, I'm afraid . . . I'm not hungry. Don't look at me like that! I'll make it up at luncheon, I promise you. Go ahead and serve the Misses MacLellan; I'll start on the upstairs hall in a minute. I want to look around here first."

She looked doubtful at that, checking the shadows one more time as if for an hostile shade before thumping down the stairs and shutting the door quietly behind her. How dear she was to have my welfare so much at heart, and how innocent to think that harm awaited me in the cluttered, gloomy attic.

How could either of us know that the danger lurked in the empty, well-lit hallway below?

It was the same hallway it had always been, with dark board floors and a drugget runner beneath dirty beams and plaster walls. I had placed extra lamps up here against the grey of the weather, since the small windows at either end admitted no light on this wet and murky day. The rain still fell in slow tedium against the glass.

As I descended from the attic, I was preoccupied with the disappearance of Duncan's case; I had an idea of taxing the aunts with it—and with the annoyance of my missing belongings —but had no inkling that my life was imperiled.

I was conscious only of blackness dropping over my head like a bag (which indeed it proved to be, made of aged black velvet, for I found it neatly folded under my head when once again I regained my senses) and of strong arms forcing me backwards. Being neither small nor weak, I naturally struggled, a course of action which availed me nothing save a sharp pain at the back of my head and an all-encompassing darkness.

My next awareness was of pain, and for a moment I was transported back to that dark road where I had lain injured under the stars, only this time there was no Simon Fordyce to ride to my rescue. There was light; had I lain there until dawn? A yellow dawn . . . How strange . . .

The second time I opened my eyes, my

position had shifted so that what I had thought to be dawn was only a prosaic lamp from the hallway. It sat calmly on the floor as if there had been no violent struggle nearby. My first thought was of gratitude that it had not tipped or been kicked over, setting the house alight. After seeing the attic I was all too conscious of what a firetrap this neglected old building had become. My second thought was of a deep thankfulness that my attacker had left me a light at all, for the small chamber in which I lay was windowless, and without the lamp the darkness would have been absolute.

My throat constricted. What if I were no longer in Jura House at all? The lamp was of common design; presumably there were hundreds of them in the valley. This was a part of the house—assuming that I was still in the house—that I had not seen before. It was a small room, not over six feet square, and totally bare of furniture. The plaster between the beams had never been smoothed and its roughness was hung with dirt and cobwebs.

I sat up—slowly, out of deference to my aching head—and looked around the bare prison with wonder. What sort of place was this? If it were a storage cupboard there should be shelving or bins of some kind . . .

And a door. As I looked around, it became obvious that every wall was the same. How on earth had I gotten in here? The ceiling and floor appeared to be as solid as the walls.

Never had I thought to be grateful to the purple-penned lady novelist; without a knowledge of her works I never would have thought of a secret passage, even when a more detailed search of the walls with the aid of the lamp revealed a crack as wide as my finger. A good tug and the panel slid open with much less resistance than I had anticipated, revealing a dark and unappealing-looking hole.

It didn't get any better inside, but there were stairs as steep and narrow as those leading to the attic. Taking the lamp, I slithered down them, trying to ignore the alarming way they creaked under my weight. Cobwebs fluttered like drapery and brushed with horrible softness against my head and shoulders. I tried to ignore the various scuttlings and scurryings at my feet. The passageway was so narrow that my skirts scraped the walls, accumulating Heaven only knew how much filth and grime.

At the moment, it seemed it would have been better to have stayed in the room and screamed. I had considered that, and rejected the idea; I did not know for sure that anyone who might hear me was necessarily friendly, or even that I was still within the house itself. Besides, the thought of so loud a sound in that confined area made my poor head ache even worse.

Now I was not so sure. The steps had ended in a tunnel so low that I was forced to stoop, bringing my face that much closer to the cobwebs and their inhabitants as well as causing a shower of loose dirt to fall about my head and shoulders. Underfoot the ground was starting to get wetter. It had been damp since the stairs had ended, but now great gouts of water lay in oily black puddles.

In that position I couldn't have missed the handkerchief; it was startlingly white against the muddy floor of the tunnel. My dress was already ruined, but I gave it no thought as I knelt to pick up what proved to be a handkerchief of the finest linen embroidered with a simple F in the corner.

Simon Fordyce.

I felt as if I had been struck. It had been easy to dismiss Dougal's accusations as jealousy, but this was evidence I could not discount so easily. I was surprised at how much it hurt; I had believed in his honor so deeply . . .

Had I allowed myself to think, doubtless I would have reached the same conclusions that I did some time later, but at the moment all I could feel was fear for my life and profound disappointment. I stuffed the handkerchief in my pocket and forged on. The tunnel seemed very unstable, and it was all too easy to picture it collapsing around my ears. At least that proved that the room in which I had awakened had another entrance; no one could have carried a prone body in through this way. Besides, my clothing had been dry when I awoke and I felt positive I had not been unconscious long enough for them to dry after such a soaking as they would have received in the tunnel.

Never had I thought that cold, grey rain from a leaden sky could look so good. The tunnel, after going on seemingly forever, ended abruptly in a tumble of rocks and brush. Leaving the lamp, I forced my way out through the scratchy gorse—much to the detriment of my dress—and looked around. Already my teeth were chattering.

I was below the garden. At the top of the scree that hid the tunnel's entrance perched the crumbling garden wall, and not far behind that, through the tangle of plants run riot, lay Jura House.

Home.

* * * * *

They had been searching for me. When I had turned up missing and no amount of looking had provided any clue to my whereabouts, Mrs. Docherty had not blamed it on the fearsome Old Ones, but had instead instituted a thorough, organized search of the house from attic to cellar. Miss Agatha had been somewhat skeptical, but Miss Jessie, bless her heart, had feared for me and would have participated had her sister not forbidden it.

When they became convinced I was not in the house, Dougal had been sent for and apprised of the situation. He had been on the brink of calling out the crofters for a full-scale search when I appeared at the door, drenched and filthy.

My condition made no difference to Dougal; he swept me into his arms and held me tightly, murmuring my name again and again. His clothing was nearly as wet as mine and there were great, muddy bootprints where he had paced up and down the floor.

"My God, Linnet! Where have you been? You had us half scared to death!"

I leaned against him, borrowing his strength as a vine borrows from a tree. Surely it could not be wrong to pretend for a moment that it was Duncan who held me, Duncan who worried about me,

Duncan who would look after me, though if Dougal had not had his brother's face it would have been difficult to conjure up a picture of my late husband, for the image that filled my mind was that of Simon Fordyce.

"There will be time enough for Linnet to explain her extraordinary actions later," Miss Agatha said authoritatively. "Now perhaps you will get out of those wet clothes and dry down before you catch your death! It's bad enough that you ride the fields like a common overseer without making yourself sick in the process! Linnet had better change, too," she added as an afterthought.

Mrs. Docherty maided me herself. She had detached me from Dougal's grip and braced my shaky trip upstairs with her own body, saving me the humiliation of being carried up like a sack of meal. There were never any fires upstairs save in the aunts' sitting room, and in anticipation of their exile to the ground-floor parlor for the duration of the cleaning, it had been left unlit. I thought my teeth would chatter right out of my head.

Standing me in the middle of the floor, Mrs. Docherty ruthlessly stripped away my sodden clothing, then wrapped me in a blanket and began to rub and pummel me until I thought her intent on taking my skin off. It was warming, though, and by the time Lois brought up a steaming can of hot water with which to wash off the worst of my accumulated grime, my teeth had ceased their chattering and my skin was a healthy pink.

During her ministrations Mrs. Docherty was oddly silent, and I could not help wondering if she had expected never to see me again. How would she report to Simon Fordyce that his plan had failed and that I was alive?

Even with the evidence in my dress pocket, why couldn't I believe that Simon Fordyce was my mortal enemy? Was I as bedazzled as Dougal had said?

Wrapped in my blanket, I waited for Mrs. Docherty to leave; she, however, had other ideas. As if I had been one of her own daughters she stripped off the blanket and sponged away my dirt herself, clucking with dismay over the scratches and bruises I had accumulated. Her motherly ministrations made short work of any embarrassment I felt, and it was pleasant to be treated as a child, especially after the strain of the last months.

"Poor darling," she muttered. "Scraped yer arm raw, ye have ... Tis a crying shame, it is, and especially as there be some who nae value ye as they should . . ."

I could not believe she was anything but what she appeared, a good and simple woman who was concerned about her employer. Of course, she could be used by that man who held her loyalty . . .

Once more I saw in memory's eye his face, as it had appeared that first night bending over me in concern, then as it had been later when the doctor had been doing his unholy work on me, and later still when it had glowed with purpose as he had described his dream of a textile mill on the Cardoc Gorge. Surely such a man would not use dishonorable methods to further his ends.

Somehow I wanted so much to believe . . .

Chapter 14

N ow," demanded Miss Agatha in clipped tones, "suppose you tell us what is behind your extraordinary behavior, Linnet?"

We were sitting in the ground-floor parlor. Dougal and I had changed into dry clothes and at Miss Jessie's insistence were seated by the fire to ward off possible chills. The Docherty girls had been busy during our time upstairs, for the polished wood floor now bore no traces of muddy footprints, and a positively sumptuous tea decorated the table. The scones were hot and smelled delicious. What a pity Miss Agatha's attitude all but curdled the butter.

I accepted a cup of tea and a scone from Miss Jessie and tried to take comfort from her smile. It was amazing how Miss Agatha could make me feel so guilty when I was obviously the victim.

"I was attacked," I said slowly.

Miss Agatha sniffed eloquently. "That seems to be a habit with you, Linnet. In truth, I do not know what we did for excitement before you came."

"Aggie, dear, don't you think that's a little . . ." Miss Jessie began, but was quelled by a speaking glance from her sister.

"I think that will be all," Miss Agatha said dismissively to Mrs. Docherty. "We do not discuss family matters before servants."

What Miss Agatha said was entirely proper; it was just the way in which she said it. I could not think that Mrs. Docherty would care to be included in our conversation, but she began to bristle at such a curt dismissal. I intervened.

"One moment, please. I would like Mrs. Docherty to be present."

Doubtless Miss Agatha took this as yet another example of my unsuitability to be a MacLellan, but a frown from Dougal kept her comments down to one bitter harrumph.

"Won't you tell us what happened, Linnet?" Dougal asked softly.

"I assure you I find it difficult to credit myself, but I was attacked." Despite the waves of remembered fear I tried to speak calmly. Hysteria would not help my case. "As you say, Miss Agatha, that has become quite a habit since my arrival. I can only hope that you do not offer such treatment to all newcomers, for I can promise you that nothing like this ever happened to me in London!"

She sat forward with flashing eyes. "That is outside of enough, miss! Dare you to accuse us . . ."

"I'm sure that Linnet did not mean to sound accusing, Aunt Agatha," Dougal said hastily. "Linnet, exactly what did happen?"

As unemotionally as possible I told of my

adventures, not at all cheered by a flicker of comprehension that passed between my relatives. When I had finished Miss Agatha daintily wiped her mouth free of crumbs and looked coldly at me.

"I see. As usual you have made a great to-do over nothing. Doubtless it was an unpleasant experience, but hardly anything to cause such a trouble over, especially since it was most likely your own fault."

"Her own fault!" Mrs. Docherty cried. She had been building up a full head of righteous steam during my recital and Miss Agatha's calm dismissal of my plight, and could hold her peace no longer. "The poor bairn's scraped raw and cut to bits. Ye canna be thinking she'd be doing that to herself!"

She might not have spoken for all the attention Miss Agatha paid her. "The room you found is an old priest's hole. At one time Jura House fell into the unfortunate grip of those disgraceful Papists, and they used it to circumvent the laws of man and the decency of God by hiding those who would spread their filth among our people. We no longer use the room, though it is hardly a secret."

"I knew nothing of it," I returned hotly.

"Obviously," was her dry reply.

"It was an oversight, I'm sure," Dougal said. He put his teacup down and crossed the small distance between our chairs to clasp my hand in his. "No one has thought of the old priest's hole in years."

"There's supposed to be another one," Miss

Jessie said dreamily. "All the old legends say there was another one, where the last priest starved to death rather than betray himself to the law . . ."

"Shut up, Jessie," snapped her sister. "That's just a silly old story with which to frighten children and servants. There never has been a second priest's hole. As for Linnet, I know what happened."

She could have thought of no better way to gain our attention. Every eye was focused on her and she took full advantage of it as she slowly fixed herself another cup of tea.

"Suppose you enlighten us, Aunt Agatha," Dougal suggested at last. He had not loosed my hand from his comforting clasp.

"I should think that would be self-evident, Dougal. During her assault on this house, she accidentally activated the mechanism which opens the door. Once inside she was unable to open it again, and rather than call for help she found the way out through the old tunnel and concocted this whole fantastic story to draw attention to herself. It would have been better to admit your foolishness and call for help, Linnet; I am surprised the old tunnel is still passable. I thought it had been closed years ago." She was unbearably superior.

I could scarcely speak for fury, and only Dougal's comforting hand kept me from doing something unacceptable, wild and utterly satisfying, like flinging my teacup at Miss Agatha.

"And the black bag that was put over my

head? And the lamp that was left for me? And this lump where I was struck?"

Her glance was frosty. "The lamp supports my point of view, for if an attacker had existed he would scarcely have left you such a comfort. We have only your word for the black bag, since you imprudently neglected to bring it with you. As for the lump on your head, that could easily have been acquired during your trip through the tunnel—which from your disgraceful condition I do not doubt you did make—or more likely it was self-inflicted in a bid for our sympathies."

"Don't you think that is a rather harsh judgment, Aunt Agatha?" Dougal began, but I could no longer be restrained by the gentle pressure of his hand.

"That is a poisonous accusation!"

"Is it? I should think that yours is the worse, Linnet. If there were an attacker, how could he get into the house itself? I doubt seriously that anyone knows of the old tunnel entrance, let alone is foolish enough to try it. Unless, of course, you are accusing one of us?"

"I accuse no one," I replied a moment later after biting back my original comments. "I am only stating facts. As for the attacker getting into the house, I say he got in the same way he did when he invaded my room, and the same way he does when I hear footsteps moving about at night! Perhaps he comes in through the tunnel! I don't know."

"Preposterous!" said Miss Agatha.

"Do you hear them, too? I think they are spirits of our ancestors, trying to get us back to the Castle." Almost lost under the thunder of angry words, Miss Jessie's voice was full of wonder, though at the time I was too far gone in anger to take in the full import of her words and they were overridden by emotion, to be recovered in memory much later.

"Jessie, you are a fool," Miss Agatha pronounced coldly. "and you, miss, are either hysterical or mentally deficient. I do not know why it should be the fate of all the men in this family to marry Southron women who are obviously unstable!"

"Please, Aunt Agatha! Linnet, if you left the black bag in the priest's hole it should still be there . . ."

"Really, Dougal, I should think your wits have gone a-wandering! If there is such an object in the hidden room, there is still no evidence that it was used on her. In fact, seeing it might have given her the idea for the whole charade!"

She was convincing him; I could see it in the way his face hardened. "Linnet . . . Don't you have any proof?"

I looked away, sure that he would see the duplicity in my eyes. How could I face him and tell him no, when the one piece of incontrovertible, damning evidence lay damply in my pocket at that exact moment? I had salvaged it from my ruined dress, taking care that Mrs. Docherty should not see it. No one should see it until I cared to show it to them.

At the time I didn't know why I hesitated, especially when Dougal stood by so protectively, waiting for my words as if he knew there was something else, something I was withholding from him. I tried to tell myself it was only for Dougal's protection that I stayed quiet, for as soon as I showed him the handkerchief and its accusing monogram he would be off to the Castle for vengeance . . . *And*, I thought, *what chance would he have against Simon Fordyce's iron muscles and hard fists?*

"No," I said at last. "Only my word, and it seems worthless here. You didn't even believe me when my Bible disappeared . . ."

"Are you back to harping on that again?" Miss Agatha snapped. "As I recall, it showed up under your bed, where you probably dropped it!"

"Yes, it showed up again, but my handkerchiefs haven't, and now Duncan's case is missing too!"

That caused all the outcry I could have wanted, and by the time the whole story was out, through Dougal's gentle probing and Miss Agatha's acid comments, I was almost in tears. It was too much for any one person to bear; I would leave, I would go back to London, I would emigrate . . . Anything to get away from Jura House and the problems of the MacLellans!

"Linnet, why haven't you told us any of this before?"

I could not meet Dougal's eyes. "Why should

I? You don't believe me, even now!"

"Without proof . . ."

The handkerchief in my pocket burned my conscience as if it were afire. Why couldn't I just hand it over to Dougal and be done with it?

Because, I thought later after fleeing to my room in tears, *Simon Fordyce was no fool*. I could see him—if indeed it was he who had been my attacker, which I had begun to doubt — leaving me a lamp for comfort, but I could not see him leaving the tunnel doorway open if he wanted me to stay there. And if he wanted me to escape through the tunnel, why had he committed the ultimate folly of losing a handkerchief there? He would never be so careless; it was almost as if he wanted to convict himself . . . or as if someone wanted to point the finger of blame at him.

But who?

And how?

And most of all, why?

All of which got me exactly nowhere except to aggravate my already aching head. I could not bring myself to indict my enigmatic, maddening neighbor, but neither could I vindicate him. All I knew was that he haunted my dreams.

For three days my life was calm. Dougal cosseted me with attentions I found just short of claustrophobic, while the aunts regarded me with the wary care one extended to temperamental animals and madmen. Only the Dochertys treated me as if they believed me wholeheartedly, and even they avoided the subject, keeping to the safe conversational areas of the progressing housecleaning and the monotony of the rainy weather.

On the fourth day the weather broke, after a fashion; the skies were still grey, but there was a hint of light behind the grey, and the rain stopped. I decided it was time I found out a few things for myself, with no influence from either side. I dressed warmly for walking and, after Dougal had left and the aunts retreated to their sitting room, walked out of Jura House into the rain-fresh air.

It took me quite a while to reach the Bruce croft on foot, not even counting the time I wasted on the wrong paths. Nothing seemed to have changed, from the messy surroundings to Mrs. Bruce's hostile attitude to the empty eyes of the children clinging to her skirts. She opened the door only a little in answer to my knock and regarded me with a flat stare.

"Good morning, Mrs. Bruce. I am Mrs. Duncan MacLellan . . . We met the other day . . ."

"I ken who ye be. What be ye a-wanting?"

I knew very little about the normal attitude of tenants to their landlord, but this hardly seemed to be it. I smiled more broadly. "I'd like to talk to you, if I may."

She opened the door and gestured me in. "Us sorry I am to be unable to offer ye a proper tea . . ." She too pronounced it "tay" and her voice dripped with sarcasm.

If possible, the place looked poorer than it

had before. Despite the chill, no fire burned in the grate and the table was bare of cutlery. A sick, dank odor hung in the house, composed of the stench of unwashed bodies and the unidentifiable but unmistakable smell of poverty.

"Sit ye down. It's the best we have," Mrs. Bruce added bitterly, gesturing to the rude settle before the cold grate.

"Thank you. Mrs. Bruce, I've come to you for help . . ."

Her bark of laughter was short and brittle. "Ye comes to me? Fine day that is!"

"Mam," cried one of the bolder children, "be this the queen what's come to live at the big house?"

My heart constricted. Was that how they thought of me? "No, dear," I said gently. "The only queen on this island lives in London. I'm just a woman trying to find out what is the best thing to do."

The child was too shy to speak to me, but Mrs. Bruce's face seemed to thaw somewhat. Like a wary animal she pulled up a stool and sat opposite me, the children clustering around her like a cloud.

"I don't know how much the valley people know about it, but Duncan left me the respon- sibility . . ."

Her eyes were like opaque glass. "It's been spoken of."

"Mr. Fordyce . . ."

That roused her! The lined face contorted. "Him! The Devil's spawn, he is! Nae MacLellan worthy of the name would breathe the same air he do!"

"A great number of people have told me that, but no one has yet told me why!" I cried.

"Why? Me bairns be hungry because of that man! Aye, and most of the families in the valley, too! 'Twas talk of killing him once, after Campbell's barn burned . . ." Here I made a small squeak of horror, but Mrs. Bruce continued animatedly. "But the dominie said 'twould come down hard on us. Them that has can step on them that hasna, but them that hasna must bear."

"What has Mr. Fordyce done?"

"Burned our barns, trampled our crops . . . if he canna get his mill built here he'll starve the valley out! Master Dougal says he'll see us protected, but . . ." Her fiery oratory faltered and died. With work-worn hands she caressed the thin faces of the two littlest children. Her voice was soft. "It be hard, mistress, and the childer gets hungry."

"Tell me, Mrs. Bruce; is the farming good in this area? Have you always been this poor?"

Thin shoulders lifted in a shrug. "Good year or bad, poor people stays poor. What God don't take, the master do."

Such fatalism wrenched at me. Duncan, my heart cried, *Duncan, what am I to do?*

My prayers were not answered; I hadn't really expected them to be. Instead, I raised my head and plodded on the best I knew how.

"Have there been many good years?"

"Nae . . . land be poor hereabouts; too poor for sheep but nae too poor for men," she added bitterly.

"Please, Mrs. Bruce, I'm asking you in confidence . . . Would you and the other women on the valley like to have a steady income?"

"Steady income?" Even the words were alien to her mouth. "Siller regular? Enough to feed all the bairns?"

"Yes."

The glow of hope in her face hurt my eyes.

"Twould be a regular gift from Heaven, mistress. Sometimes the childer cry with hunger . . ."

"So if a mill were built . . ."

That was the wrong thing to say; once again the ravaged face was lit with righteous anger. "We'd burn it to the ground! We be poor in the valley, but we nae canna be bought with a Southron's siller! Working for him would be little better than slavery!"

The words sounded familiar. "Who told you that?"

"Master Dougal, of course. Last month he told me man we wasna to worrit our heads about such, that there would be siller for everybody and plenty to bring the land to life again." Her trust in the master's word seemed absolute.

And how could Dougal speak so definitely more than a month ago of the way the inheritance should be spent? I thought hard, piecing it together.

He probably expected that Duncan would follow his line of thinking about using the inheritance to rejuvenate the family holdings, I decided; even if he had made the statement after Duncan's death, Dougal would have had no way of knowing at that time that the inheritance would pass to me. Still, I had been here almost a month . . .

What had Duncan wanted?

"Be ye all right, mistress?"

I snapped back to the present, embarrassed at being caught so flagrantly daydreaming. "Forgive me, Mrs. Bruce. I was just thinking . . ."

"'Twas sure sorrowful yer man died along so sudden-like," she said, straining in an effort to make polite conversation. "He were well thought of hereabouts, he were."

"Everyone liked Duncan," I murmured. It struck me with a sudden and uncomfortable force that everyone in this valley, including Simon Fordyce, had known my husband longer than I had, and by now I had spent almost the same amount of time in Dougal's company as in Duncan's. The revelation left me strangely hollow.

By the time I had extricated myself from Mrs. Bruce's clumsy attempts at sociability, it was well past luncheon time; I had no idea if the Bruce household had the luxury of a luncheon meal, but did not intend to put them to the ill-afforded extravagance of asking me to join them. Apparently Mrs. Bruce had recovered sufficiently from the initial bad impression of seeing me with Simon Fordyce to accept me as lady of the manor. I have little acquaintance with the interaction between tenants and landlords, but I found her obsequiousness positively irritating. The MacLellans were not royalty, no matter what airs they gave themselves.

Hoofbeats sounded dully on the road behind me, awakening reverberations within my mind of those other hoofbeats on the darkened road to Jura House. To fall once more under those sharp, plunging hooves, to feel again the Archangel's wings as he came to carry my spirit away . . . Perhaps such memories were only fancies born of pain and darkness and terror, but they were enough to send me jumping onto the grassy verge without conscious volition.

"Linnet! I'm sorry!" Dougal yanked his horse to a slithering stop. "I didn't mean to frighten you. Didn't you hear me calling?"

With as much dignity as possible, I walked back onto the roadway, fully aware of the ridiculousness of my actions and quite thankful that I had not gone so far as to fling myself full length in the ditch.

"No, I didn't, Dougal. I was just lost in thought . . . You startled me."

Instantly he was out of the saddle and walking beside me, one hand negligently holding his horse's reins, the other under my elbow. I rather wished he would use both hands to control his mount should it decide to become frisky. At best I was timorous of the great beasts.

"I crave your forgiveness," he said, as one sure of receiving it. "You have picked a singularly dreary area for a walk. The views to the back of the house are much more amusing."

"I came this way in hopes of talking to some of the crofters. Duncan would have wanted me to get to know these people."

"They all loved Duncan . . . looked to him like some sort of savior. The young master; that's what they called him. Poor sod, to have that much pinned on him since his cradle days . . ." Despite his disparaging tones Dougal could not keep a shade of envy out of his voice. It must have been hard on him, seeing the expectations and honors heaped on one who was his exact duplicate save for the accident of having been born only minutes earlier.

"I wish we could find Duncan's case," I said suddenly, tears welling in my eyes. "If only I knew what he would have wished me to do!"

Suddenly Dougal hugged me to him with a tenderness he had never before shown. "I miss him, too, Linnet. Between twins like us there is a special bond . . . I feel almost as if a part of myself has died." For a moment his voice was dangerously tense as he said, "In his memory we must do the best we can for this valley. We must build the MacLellan name back to the glory it once had!"

I could think of nothing to say to this, but there was no need. Dougal swallowed his melancholy mood as abruptly as shutting a door and swung up into the saddle.

"Come, Linnet! It is late and our tea will be waiting. Give me your hand . . ."

From my viewpoint he looked impossibly high, silhouetted up there against the metallic sky. Only once before had I ridden like that; Simon Fordyce had swept me up into his arms and carried me like a child.

"I do not mind walking, Dougal. It is not very far . . ."

"Nonsense! I shall not let you fall, believe me. Come, Linnet . . . Give me your hand and put your foot there on the stirrup and . . . Up you come!"

It was not as simple as it sounded; it took a great deal of effort to get me safely seated across the bow of his saddle, an endeavor complicated by the fact that the docile-looking brown horse objected to such an unfamiliar load and showed his displeasure by dancing about in a most irritated way. Once lodged in reasonable security on the horse's shoulders, I clung to Dougal in a manner more suited to some sort of parasitic vine. I had not remembered that horses were so tall and felt so unstable. Dougal at least was solid and safe, though it was impossible to compare his encircling arms, slender almost to the point of delicacy, to the massive strength and musculature of Simon Fordyce, in whose arms I had last ridden like this.

As if my thoughts had conjured him up like a djinn, from this vantage point I could see him watching us from the far hillside across the burn. Despite the distance it was obvious that he could be no other, nor to mistake the disgust with which he wheeled his horse and galloped away.

Chapter 15

There was a moon that night, a poor wasted slip of a thing that played a merry game of hide-and-seek with the clouds. She searched for holes in the overcast sky to peek through, then before one's eyes could become adjusted to her light, dashed back and hid again.

Wakeful, I watched the lightspill from her games appear and disappear on the newly polished floor. Even in the fitful moonlight my room glistened and gleamed like something new-made. It was a consolation to realize that with the exception of the aunts' suite and the attic, the entire house was now scrubbed and waxed, though whatever vague goal my frantic activity had striven to attain remained as distant and nebulous as ever. The fulfillment of scrubbing and cleaning had faded with the cessation of activity, leaving nothing to fill the hollow void of my being but the comforts of a clean house and good cooking and the knowledge that the ancient Mrs. Giles had been decently pensioned off.

Doubtless I should begin to feel useful again once we started the rejuvenation of the valley, but that would entail making a decision for which I was not qualified. Farm or mill? Farm or mill? The litany repeated again and again in my brain, gnawing away at my peace until I lay awake and fretful. At least I tried to pretend it was such a lofty problem and ignore the scalding blush that seared my soul each time I remembered the way Simon Fordyce had galloped away after seeing me with Dougal, as if he could not quit the air shared with us quickly enough.

What was Simon Fordyce to me?

I struggled with the bedclothes and changed to another, equally uncomfortable position.

Why should he occupy so much of my thoughts? He was a strong, selfish man who appeared capable of using any means to forward his own ends, yet I could not force myself to believe what was apparently common knowledge in the valley.

Why did my pulse race uncontrollably when he turned those lazy blue eyes on me? Why should I scarcely be able to recall Duncan's face had not his twin been living in the house with me?

I had loved Duncan. He had been kind and gentle and giving, and surely my appreciation of those qualities was the hallmark of love rather than the turbulence within my being that characterized my reaction to Simon Fordyce. Mother had spoken wistfully of the security of love, whose reality she had never known; security Duncan had offered in plenty, but in the wild tumult aroused in me by the man from the Castle was no thought of security or even safety.

What was this untamed and primitive country

doing to me?

My thoughts ended abruptly, cut off by the muffled sound of footsteps below. Quick and irregular, as if having more thought for speed than for concealment, they floated gently on the still night air. Had I been asleep or the rain been drumming its tattoo on the slate roof, the sounds would never have been heard.

That was a nasty thought; how many times had I slept snugly in this bed thinking myself secure, unaware of what was going on below? And for that matter, just what was going on below? If that were Mr. Simon Fordyce making himself so free of my house for whatever purpose, I would have an explanation!

I have stated before that my temper often gets the best of me and precludes rational thought; it was so that moon-haunted night. I slipped from bed, gasping only slightly as my bare feet touched the icy floor, seized the concealing drabness of my everyday shawl, and crept out into the hallway. Even if my slippers had been to hand I should not have stopped for them; their hard soles would have made far too much noise, and by now my feet could not get any colder.

Silently I slid down the corridor, following the receding lure of sound, doubtless the most solid and corporeal wraith ever to walk the halls of our less than stately home. At that moment I felt I should be able to give firsthand advice to the fanciful lady novelist. No character of hers ever desired to sneeze, nor had to stuff the fringe of her shawl into her mouth to keep the chattering of her teeth from being audible.

The house looked much bigger by moonlight; it was almost as if some magic had distorted time and space and enlarged the rooms. The cool bluish light poured into the rooms like skimmed milk, then blinked out into blackness at the whim of a passing cloud, only to return from another angle and make the room seem altogether different.

Under my frozen feet the hallway flags were rough and gritty. I moved forward slowly with only my fingertips against the wall as a guide; here beneath the stairs the darkness was profound and out of range of the moon's questing fingers. From a spot almost under my fingers there was a sharp click, and then a silence in which I could hear my heart beating.

I am ashamed to admit it, but at that moment my nerve broke. The darkened hallway was populated with every nursery horror I had ever heard of, and each was waiting with teeth and claws . . . I ran, looking more wraithlike than ever with my shawl and nightrail belling out from haste and my hair streaming loose from its soft nighttime braid. My feet were silent on the old floor, and in the moon-blessed haven of my room the only sound was that of my labored breathing.

I must have stood there for some minutes with my back against the door as if to repel some determined intruder until the soft creaking of a board once more drew my wandering wits into focus. The considerate moon had hidden her face once more and I ventured on her generosity enough to open the door a crack.

Save for the talkative floorboard there was no sound, but since wraiths and spirits do not need candles, I surmised that it was indeed the figure of Miss Jessie who flowed past me down the hall and into her own room. So I was not the only nocturnal prowler! Miss Jessie was a harmless enough spectre compared to the horrors that had populated my imaginings, but that did not explain why she should walk so silently up here and yet sound like a crowd below.

My determination to tax Miss Jessie with her midnight activities the next morning was sidetracked most definitely. The aunts normally breakfasted late, a relic of the old days when as pampered daughters of an indulgent father they had made their own rules. In my early isolation even though I did not care for breakfast as a meal I had formed the habit of taking a cup of tea early, more as a way of avoiding their hostility than through any personal inclination, so it was with some surprise that I received their invitation to join them in the dining room. Under such circumstances it would have been churlish to refuse to partake of the meal, so I forced down a bowl of porridge. It was even more of a surprise to find Dougal, who was usually up and abroad before any of us stirred, waiting there to present me with what to his mind was a most magnificent surprise. He seemed hurt when I could not share his excitement.

"A what?"

"A horse. After finding you on the road yesterday I realized what a selfish creature I have become. As the mistress of Jura House and the widow of Duncan MacLellan you should be properly mounted; too much can happen when you walk," he added darkly.

How well I knew that, but horseback riding seemed little safer, and I said so.

"That's where I've been selfish, Linnet. As a MacLellan . . . the MacLellan of the valley . . . it's important that you ride; the crofters expect it. They can't respect anyone who gets about no better than they."

That seemed shaky logic, but Dougal went on, giving me no chance for a rebuttal.

"I've been using both horses and not seen to it that you're properly mounted. I told myself that you were busy with the house and there was time, but when I saw you on the road the other day, the hem of your dress all draggled and mucky as any crofter's . . . It made me ashamed, it did."

His penitence was so obvious I could not help saying, "It's all right . . ."

"Then you forgive me, and we can start your lessons today!" he crowed with delight, slapping the table so hard that the breakfast dishes jiggled gently.

"Wait, I didn't say that . . ."

"It is expected that the MacLellans ride," Miss Agatha spat. Obviously my reluctance to risk life and limb on a horse was another black mark against my character.

"When we lived at home there was a stable," Miss Jessie said. The edges of her mouth were rimmed with creamy porridge as if with paint. "We used to ride every day. I loved to ride . . . To gallop across the open moors and then to jump the burn . . ." Her old face glowed with an inner animation. "It was like flying."

Such reminiscences were hardly the kind to induce me to enthusiasm. To entrust oneself to the caprices of a beast without the protection of a carriage seemed the utmost foolhardiness. I knew that there were people and even ladies who rode well and enjoyed it, but it seemed that without exception they had been brought up around horses and learned to master them before learning the wisdom of fear.

"You never jumped the burn in your life, Jessie MacLellan! Dear Papa spent his life trying to make a decent rider out of you," her sister growled. "It was I who won the ribbon two years running at the County Show!"

Somehow the ghost of the prideful girl who had won at the horse show glimmered palely in the ravaged face of Agatha MacLellan. What might her life have been had her father not been a gambling wastrel and her brother a cowardly weakling unable to face life?

The waste, the waste . . .

My charitable mood lasted only a few seconds, until she spoke again.

"The ability to ride is the mark of a lady. Had you forgotten that, Dougal? We must not expect too much of Linnet."

"That's going a bit far, Aunt Agatha . . ."

"The ability to ride is the mark of those who have the money to afford it," I said bitterly. "I have yet to see that money alone can substitute for good breeding."

Either she was more controlled than I had given her credit for or my barb went completely past her, for Miss Agatha, deliberately withdrawn from the conversation as much as if she had left the room, merely nodded absently and continued to sugar her second helping of porridge.

"Come riding with me, Linnet," Dougal pleaded. "I know it's what Duncan wanted, for his last letter was full of plans to find a suitable mount for you . . ."

How long could I hold out against such gentle pleading in the name of my lost husband, especially when the eyes and voice were so like his? "I have no habit . . ." I floundered weakly.

"This is not London, where the modes dictate all," Dougal replied brightly. "Of course you must have a habit, but just for a gentle ride over the country to the south . . . what you have on will do until you learn." Deprecatingly his hand swept toward my dress. Of course it was an old one dyed black for my mourning, but it was of heavy material and old-fashioned in cut. "The skirts are big enough to fit over the saddle."

"A side-saddle . . ."

"Doubtless he intends to put you on mine," Miss Agatha snapped, all pretence of distance gone, sounding as if I had personally engineered the usurpation of her property. "It is the best that could be bought."

"I remember I rode astride once," Miss Jessie mumbled between mouthfuls of porridge. "I stole James's saddle and breeches and rode to the Campbells' farm . . . Mama was so scandalized, and Papa whipped me until I couldn't sit for a week . . ."

"Shut up, Jessie! You never rode astride in your life. It was I who borrowed James's saddle and breeches."

The spectacle of a young Agatha riding astride over the countryside was too much for my poor mind to encompass.

"Why, Aggie dear, that's just not true! I still remember how Papa was chuckling with pride even while he was spanking me, calling me his young Valkyrie!"

"It was always I whom Papa called his young Valkyrie! You never did anything but sit with Mama and look at dress patterns!"

Though her oatmeal-daubed lower lip quivered with repressed indignation, Miss Jessie lowered her eyes and defiantly added more sugar to her already twice-sweetened porridge. Both aunts had decried my efforts to improve the fare at Jura House, but neither had boycotted the table and both had developed a decided partiality to sweets.

"I've ordered Duncan's horse saddled for you, Linnet," Dougal said seductively. "Come with me."

I'm not quite sure how he did it, yet the next thing I knew I was being bundled in one of Duncan's old winter cloaks and handed somewhat ungracefully onto what was perhaps the biggest animal ever born. Dougal had said that Duncan's horse was gentle and easy to ride; his rolling eyes and nervous hooves belied this and Dougal's assurances that Laird's Pride was only reacting to my own nervousness. I had been hoping for a fat, sluggish cob, the kind on which three-year-olds are safely placed, not this enormous mass of ill-contained energy.

"All right, Linnet. This foot goes here and your hand here; now when I throw you up into the saddle, you loop your right limb about the horn and settle this foot in the stirrup . . . It's easy."

"It certainly doesn't sound so, or even safe. What do you mean, throw me up into the saddle?"

His smile was encouraging. "Trust me." Bending over, he interlaced his fingers to form into a cup. "Step here and . . . up you go!"

On the fourth try I finally landed more or less in the saddle and, with Dougal's help arranged myself into the accepted equestrienne position. Of the previous three tries only one had managed to get me anywhere near the accursed beast; I could almost hear the aunts laughing from their vantage point behind the parlor curtains.

"There!" Dougal puffed. "Feel secure?" By now I was quite sure that he was as heartily sick of the project as I was.

"No. It's too high up and I feel most dreadfully unprotected . . . I don't like this, Dougal."

With an enviable ease he swung up onto his own mount, whom I could not help feeling was commiserating or perhaps conspiring with my baleful-eyed steed.

"It's strange at first, but everyone feels that way when they're learning. I remember Duncan and I used to fall off regularly."

I found that singularly uncheering, but was given no opportunity to say so, for at that moment Laird's Pride decided that this would be a good time to test the mettle of his new rider by dancing to the side in dainty little steps. I failed miserably, yanking the reins so tightly that the horse's head was all but pulled back in my lap. Laird's Pride took offense at such unsportsmanlike treatment and began to set about removing this irritant—me—in earnest.

Only Dougal's quick action saved me. Leaning out at a seemingly impossible angle from his own mount, he grabbed the reins, and as much by the force of his will as by his grip compelled Laird's Pride to be still.

"Good God, Linnet! Never yank a horse's head like that! Pride has a sensitive mouth . . . You could hurt him."

This all but confirmed my contention that the MacLellans were mad. "I? Hurt him?"

"Yes! Easy boy; easy . . . it's all right . . ." Dougal then angered me further by crooning to the ill-tempered beast much as a sentimental mother might babble to a very young baby. It seemed to work, however, for Pride ceased his fidgeting and stood quite still, with only an occasional twitch of a muscle to make sure my reflexes were in good order.

"Dougal, I don't want to do this."

"Nonsense! Once you get over your first fright you'll love it," he replied with the heartiness of one who could conceive of no other course. "You see, a good horse has a very tender mouth . . . You must be very gentle with them, because hard-mouthed animals tend to be meaner and more difficult to control."

My look at him was eloquent but wasted, and I could spare no thought to a suitable verbal rebuttal; my entire energy was concentrated on staying on top of this dizzying perch and trying to forget how far it was to the hard ground. I locked my right ankle under my left knee as Dougal had told me, gripping the large curved horn (as the limb support was called) with my right knee. My spine was curved, my right foot was going to sleep, and all in all I had seldom been more uncomfortable in my life. The idea that some women voluntarily underwent such torture for amusement was inconceivable.

"I think that until you feel a bit more secure I'd better put you on a leading rein," Dougal said with ill-disguised disgust. From his pocket he pulled a thin strip of leather, which he hooked to Pride's bridle. Even I knew that this was a training aid normally used with very small children, but at the moment fear far outweighed my puny pride. My right leg was already numb, else I would have leaped to the ground in one last burst of sanity. Then the horses were moving, and joggling and bouncing like a sack of meal I followed Dougal out of the yard.

Chapter 16

Though out of necessity I have since learned to be fairly proficient in the art of riding, the pleasure of such an exercise eludes me to this very day, a circumstance that is almost wholly blamable on that first day's experience. When I lurched out of Jura House's sagging front gate, tugged behind Dougal more like cargo than a pupil, I had no idea of the consequences. Being a Christian woman of deep faith, I like to believe that the good that eventually resulted from that fateful day's events would have occurred anyway; no one wants to think that evil can flourish without check indefinitely. It is a cornerstone of our faith that God will conquer Evil in the grand plan, and what is the grand plan but a series of recurring victories over smaller sins?

I digress. It should go without saying that at the time my mind was less on cosmic justice than the more mundane subject of keeping my all-too-corporeal self intact and uninjured. The swaying of Pride's gait—a deliberate provocation by the fiendish animal, I am convinced—churned up my stomach and the ill-advised porridge   it contained until the prospect of falling off seemed quite supportable by contrast, except that by now my death grip had wedged my limbs so deeply into the saddle's contours that such an eventuality was impossible.

To do him credit, Dougal was an excellent teacher. With a pupil who possessed more desire and aptitude than I, he could have turned out a more passable horsewoman.

I practiced on a large, open area something over a mile from Jura House. This was the beginning of the moors, that vast wasteland of earth and sky where there were no markers whatever to guide one's way. While that may be an exaggeration, it is true that people unfamiliar with the area do disappear, to be found only years later as pathetic heaps of bones, sometimes still clutching their staffs and rucksacks. I can say from personal experience that it is a wild and desolate country.

Two sides of our practice field were open to the vastness of the moors, though the vistas were blocked and dimmed by nearby groves and the thick, grey sky that seemed to sag to the ground. The northernmost boundary was a craggy wall of rock, something of a natural landmark. Beyond it ran a rough chain of hills that eventually grew into the awesome Cuillins of the North. From the side of these hills flowed the noisy burn that bustled busily down the eastern edge of the field, sometimes almost level with the ground, sometimes flowing deep in a rock-lined channel.

Dougal placed the reins in my hand with a stern order not to jerk them, then unsnapped the leading rein. I was glad to see that the ground looked soft and almost spongy.

"Are you ready, Linnet?"

For the next half hour we had an intensive lesson; by the end of that time I was exhausted and Dougal was almost as disgusted with me as Pride was. There was no doubt that that high-spirited beast was extremely put out with me; he was used to daring riders who would allow him to skim fences and gallop along roads with no thought of falling. It was probably as unnerving for him to be confined under a creature who squeaked when he twitched away an annoying insect or grabbed on for dear life when he attempted anything more than the sedatest of walks as it was for me to be perched most precariously atop a monster with a definite—and decidedly malign—mind of his own.

Dougal sighed and raised a strained face to the low sky. Grey and bloated, it hung in swags like draperies. There was a smell of rain in the air.

"Maybe that's enough for today," he said wearily. "Are you ready to turn back?"

I sighed in relief. "Yes. Very much so."

"You know, you would do much better if you weren't so afraid. Falling off is a natural part of riding . . . As mistress of the valley, you're going to have to learn. How else can you inspect the farms? There aren't that many roads where a carriage can go . . ."

Now seemed as good a time as any to tell him;

the weight of my decision had been pressing on me since I had made up my mind. Or rather, the weight of telling Dougal. During the previous night the solution to the valley's and my own problems had arrived fullblown and ready for implementation. It seemed so rational to my way of thinking that I wondered that no one had ever proposed it before; but of course, I did not then realize the selfishness that fanaticism breeds.

"I don't think it will be necessary to inspect the farms, Dougal; not for a while at least."

Dougal was not a stupid man. For a moment his eyes raked me with probing intensity as his face lapsed into an expressionless mask. I felt scoured by that gaze, as if I had done something shameful or dishonorable.

"So you have gone to Fordyce's camp," he said in a queer, strangled voice. I felt sorry for him; it must be difficult to have an ignorant interloper come from nowhere with complete power over that which he had known and loved all his life, and even more so when the power was to be used contrary to his deepest beliefs.

"No, not entirely. I think you and Mr. Fordyce have gotten so enmeshed in the conflict of personalities that the real issues have become blurred," I stammered, trying futilely to soften the blow. "The ugliness about the Castle didn't help . . ."

"The man is an interloper, Linnet! He doesn't understand the valley or its people or its traditions . . ."

"Are all traditions necessarily good?" I asked, and was rewarded with a surprisingly bitter look. "The people of the valley are our responsibility, as everyone keeps reminding me. Is a tradition of poverty and hard work and few rewards to be preferred to a chance at a brighter future?"

"He has really corrupted you," my brother-in-law spat. "The valley would have been better off if Duncan had never seen you!"

"Perhaps," I said slowly. "But he did leave me this responsibility, and I must do the best I can. Dougal, when was the last time you really looked at the farms?"

We had been walking slowly over the field. At least he had not made a move to snap back on the humiliating leading rein, so I assumed that at least some progress had been made.

"Look at the farms? I am out riding them every day!"

"I know you are, but I mean really looked at them. They're bitterly poor, Dougal, and nearly starving. The land is poor. Even in the good years the farmers don't make any money . . . There are hungry children out there! Children! There are people without any hope out there . . ."

"And selling their souls into the slavery of Fordyce's mill is going to make their lives any better? Don't be a dreamer, Linnet! The land is all that's important . . . Once you put the inheritance back into the land, the quality of our crops will rise to what it ... once was before the land was starved ... The valley will prosper again without changing any of the important ways of life."

"And if we plough the whole inheritance back into the land and it doesn't work? Where would we be then? We'd have lost everything and gained nothing. Don't you be a dreamer, Dougal. I don't intend to be," I said pridefully. Pride goeth before a fall. "I intend to be a mill owner."

"What?"

"If you and Fordyce hadn't been so busy fighting your class war and Miss Agatha hadn't made such a fuss about the Castle, you would have seen the solution yourselves. Right now the glory of the MacLellan name and the reclamation of the Castle and the fight of mill versus farm aren't important, Dougal!"

"Then what in the name of Heaven is important?" he screamed. His face was contorted with anger.

"The people of the valley. Those people are dependent on us and we've got to do the very best for them. How can you sit there complacently and talk of history and traditions when the children of the people you lead are going hungry right this minute?"

"These are hard times, especially for Scotland ..."

"And we have the ability to change that, even if just for this valley. I'm going to ask Mr. Fordyce to call, and I will offer him the land he wants as well as an investment in exchange for half-ownership of the mill. That way we'll have just as much say as he, and you won't have to worry about the horrors of slavery and low wages you've feared."

I thought it a masterly solution to an almost insoluble problem and, justifiably proud of myself, sat back and waited for his congratulations.

Dougal glared at me. "You're mad. Partnership with that base-born outsider? You would drag the name of MacLellan down to the level of a tradesman?"

"If it will feed those hungry children," I said venomously, "I would scrub the floor with it!"

"We will discuss this more later," he replied with equal emotion. "I'll talk to Cameron. My brother was under undue influence; his will must be declared invalid. He would never have wanted the family to be so humiliated by a fortune-seeking chit!"

I have never been quite sure exactly what happened next. I know I was going to make some stinging and angry reply to his hurtful words. For the first time since we had left Jura House I was not completely conscious of being perched defenseless atop a huge and unfamiliar animal; this cost me any slight chance I may have had of controlling the situation.

Without warning Dougal's horse screamed and rose up on his hind feet, twisting and fighting like a mad thing. No sooner had his hooves left the earth than Pride, not to be outdone, began to behave in a similar manner. More mindful of my safety than of his mouth, I yanked at the reins in a futile attempt to calm him, but apparently he was beyond such restraints. He shied away from Dougal's beast's flying hooves, seeking space and air to slash with his own.

Then the impossible occurred; at the height of his horse's twisting frenzy, Dougal flew from the saddle to land with a crushing thunk into a crumpled knot of arms and legs that did not move. It took only seconds for all this to happen, but I can remember screaming his name, willing that he rise from that motionless heap and save me. Only my numb thigh firmly wedged in that wretched saddle kept me from joining him.

Pride decided he had had enough. Paying no attention to my frantic screams and jerking on the reins, he wheeled, and unfolding an incredible length of leg, began to fly over the ground. Somewhere I dropped the reins —a foolish move, for if he had stepped on them at full gallop he would have gone head over heels and we both should have broken our necks. I stretched out as low as I could along his neck, entwining my fingers in his streaming mane. Below the ground flew by in a dizzying blur. He jumped the burn with a magnificent stretch and landed with a jar that instead of shaking me free only served to wedge me further into that saddle.

We were in the moor now and traveling so fast that even to get my breath was a desperate task. I had heard tales about the moor, of the bogs in which a slow and terrible death awaited the unwary and of the sudden holes where anything foolish enough to fall in was lost forever. Pride, however, had heard no such tales, and instead ran blindly on with no heed to the consequences. More frightening still, his hooves made no noise on the spongy ground. Miss Jessie had been right; it did feel as if we were flying.

I do not remember when I became aware that Pride and I were no longer alone on the moor, I only knew that suddenly a creature in a black cloak that flew outward like wings mounted huge black horse, fresher and bigger than Pride, was pulling alongside. At the time I was understandably near hysterics, and it was not until they were quite close that I recognized the black-cloaked rider as Simon Fordyce, and not Death.

With insultingly little effort he grabbed Pride's bridle and slowed both horses to a gradual stop. Then he was on the ground holding Pride's head tightly and talking the same baby-style gibberish to him that Dougal had. Beneath my shaking limbs the horse's sides heaved like a blacksmith's bellows.

"It's all right, Linnet. You can get down now."

"I can't."

"What?"

"I can't."

Instead of exhorting me to strain and do my utmost as a MacLellan, Simon Fordyce merely nodded and led the horses a short way to where a stunted tree struggled through the soil and fog. Although Pride seemed exhausted and all too happy to be still, Simon tied the dangling reins firmly to the gnarled trunk before coming back to me.

"Let go . . ." Gently he freed my fingers from the entangling mane. "Now take your foot out of here and . . . You're really stuck in there, aren't you? Might be a blessing, since that's probably why you didn't fall off and break your neck. Now let me push . . ." He grunted and shoved my limb upwards out of the horn. It was quite improper that any gentleman not her husband should lay hands on a lady's lower limbs in that familiar fashion, but by now I was past caring. With a heave I was free of the saddle's death grip and fell forward into his waiting arms.

There was water on my face.

"It's raining."

His chuckle was rich and warm. "It has been for the past few minutes. You're soaked. Are you all right?"

"I'm perfectly fine," I said in clear tones just before sliding abruptly into a dead faint.

Chapter 17

At first I thought I was back in London; there were no street sounds or smells reminiscent of the metropolis, yet there was feeling of warmth and security that I had not known since my mother and husband had died. Even though such a sense of comfort was illusory, for that reason alone I was unwilling to awaken from my dreamy half-sleep. The more aware I became of my surroundings, however, the more I realized that I was not actually comfortable at all. In fact, where I lay was exceedingly hard, and there was an aroma better suited to a stable than to a bedchamber.

My eyes flew open.

"Ah, you're awake," said Simon Fordyce. "I was beginning to be concerned about you."

It came back in a rush: the horse, the accident, my romantic rescue . . . Dougal! Hastily I babbled out my fears.

"I doubt if he's badly injured; you weren't that far from the house, so someone has probably found him by this time. Even if they haven't, you are my primary concern at this moment, Mrs. MacLellan."

Mrs. MacLellan again, even though I had a very clear memory of his calling me Linnet before. It was oddly disappointing.

We were in a croft, or to be more precise, the ruins of what had once been a croft. Later inspection proved that the roof was entirely gone and the thin shelter between us and the weeping sky was what had been the upstairs floor. Part of it was missing, allowing the elements to pour in at the other end of the room. From appearances, it would not be long before the rest would follow. Luckily our shelter was at the fireplace nook, where Simon had found enough dry debris to make a blaze that could withstand the rain hissing down the broken chimney. Other than that, the place was neglected and filthy, covered with the irrefutable evidence that the croft's last occupants had been a large herd of sheep.

I couldn't say when I had started to think of our dour neighbor as Simon instead of Mr. Fordyce or "that interloper," only that the name was strong and direct and very suitable to him.

Solemnly he stuck his hand up under my skirt. I started and pulled away, but before the intent of my movement could be completed he withdrew his hand.

"Just as I thought. Your petticoats are fairly dry. Slip off your dress and I'll put it to air." Casually he gestured to the hearth where our two cloaks already sizzled and steamed.

"Mr. Fordyce! I hardly think it proper . . ."

"You disappoint me, Mrs. MacLellan. Don't come over all maidenish and prissy with me. I assure you I have no intention of ravishing you the moment you remove your dress—if I did have such ideas, a dress wouldn't stop me. All that aside, however, your clothes are soaked and I have no intention of having you go sick on me. Now out of that dress!"

Somehow his blunt roughness was more reassuring than any number of silken pledges of respect. I nodded, and while he chivalrously made a great show of walking to the sagging doorway and studying the weather, I slipped out of the sodden ruin of my dress.

Amazingly enough, my petticoats—in preparation for riding that morning I had worn an extra two for padding, making a total of four—were fairly dry and my camisole of thick warm cotton wasn't even damp. My arms were bare, however, and at the touch of the chill air shriveled into a mass of goose-flesh.

"Here," he said and extended his riding jacket. "Put this on."

I did, and gratefully. Of course it swallowed me, but it was dry and warm from the heat of his body. It smelled of him too, a nice combination of talc and bay rum and the indefinable scent of the man himself, bringing sweeping back a memory of the first time I had lain in his arms when he had found me injured on the dark road to Jura House.

"It seems you are making a habit of saving my

life," I said softly. "How can I thank you adequately?"

"By staying off horses you can't handle," was his brusque reply.

He wore no vest and the simple cut of his linen shirt showed his musculature to advantage, as did his well-fitting breeches. I watched while he spread my dress before the fire, stifling a sharp sting of emotion as it became obvious that the intricacies of women's attire held no mystery for him.

"I assure you I would be most happy to stay off all horses forever," I replied with feeling. "I was not enthusiastic about the prospect of learning to ride at all."

He turned toward me. His expression was opaque. "Learning to ride?"

"Yes. Dougal insisted that it was my duty as lady of the house to learn. In London there was never any need . . ." Nor any money; private horses were a luxury for the wealthy of the city. Poor folk like us either rode the horse-drawn trams or walked.

"So Dougal was teaching you to ride? Good God, why did he put you on Laird's Pride?"

"He said he was Duncan's horse . . . That he would be easy to manage . . ."

Simon Fordyce uttered a single, sharp expletive, then said, "With all due respect to the late Duncan MacLellan, he could no more handle a horse like Laird's Pride than a ten-year-old child! Duncan was no great shakes as a horseman, but he knew enough to realize that a horse like that was beyond his abilities."

I swallowed, my throat suddenly dry. "Then just whom does Pride belong to?"

"To Dougal, of course. He bought the beast as soon as he came down from the university. He's the horseman in the family. Apparently always has been; even made me a decent offer for my Crusader once."

"I don't suppose the stables at Jura House have many horses," I offered lamely. "They wouldn't keep a lady's horse when no lady there rides . . ."

"No, you can't defend him that way. He has a brown animal that isn't really docile enough for a lady but would have made a much better mount for you than Laird's Pride."

"He rode a brown horse today . . . that's the one that threw him."

He snarled out a harrumph. "I didn't think the horse had been born that could throw Dougal MacLellan." He rose, his muscles working in a symphony of lithe motion that was beautiful to watch, and began to prowl the ruin for more fuel. "All I can say is that it's lucky for you I was close enough to hear you cry out. I . . . ." He stopped suddenly, leaving a profound silence.

"What is this place?" I said at last.

"An old croft. Been neglected for years, as you can see, but the family who built it must have been pretty prosperous at the time. Two floors aren't common around here."

I looked around the gutted husk and tried to

picture it as a living home. The room would be bright from the fire and there would be a smell of cooking in the air . . . I pictured the mother in blue as she bustled about with bread and bowls, assisted by a small cloud of swarming daughters. The sons sat by their father on the settle, their appetites growing as they awaited the meal. Here all were healthy and happy; there were no starveling children with hollow eyes and matchstick limbs . . .

"What became of them?"

"Who knows? Perhaps they were evicted during the clearances, or perhaps they emigrated to Australia or America in hopes of finding a better life." He flung a rain-speckled chunk of wood on the fire. It hissed and spat and steamed before the fire caught and it began to burn. "Life in this part of Scotland has never been particularly generous."

My image of the happy, well-fed family was crumbling, to be replaced by the spectral duplicates of the sad-eyed children who stalked my conscience. I clasped my hands to my eyes as if to shut out the sight of those empty eyes and empty lives. Instantly he was kneeling beside me, his arms strong and protective around me as he pulled me toward him.

"Linnet! Are you all right?"

I was going to say that I enjoyed his using my given name, but could do no more than raise my head before he was kissing me. His lips were firm and smooth, but hardly gentle; they demanded, they took, they claimed mine as their own with a triumphant fervor that was as different from Duncan's respectful caresses as chalk from cheese. I was drowning, sinking, flying . . . My arms clung to his muscular body with an ardor stronger than I had ever known, one that threatened to pull my frail will asunder.

"My God," he murmured into my hair, pulling me yet closer to him. "I've longed to do that . . . Linnet, Linnet . . ."

"Simon," I breathed in capitulation. "Simon, Simon . . . Hold me . . .

"Don't you think I've wanted to?" His voice was rough with a barely suppressed emotion that was both frightening and exhilarating. "You've driven me mad with your smile and your words and your serious, beautiful eyes . . ."

Abruptly he pushed me away, striding to the opposite side of the croft. His body was a study of untamed energy bound by chains of the spirit. He was longing to say something and I was longing to hear it, even as I loathed myself for that same longing.

I could not castigate myself severely enough. I was a widow of only a short standing, yet here I was responding to his advances with the enthusiasm of a woman of the streets. There was not even any claim of love, only a pure, raw animal power that was frightening. Any lady of breeding ought to die for shame rather than admit she felt such stirrings within her. There was no gentleness, no respect, no love such as Duncan's in Simon Fordyce's arms. I would carry to my grave the disgraceful knowledge that had he not broken the embrace I never would have, despite the cloud cast over him by that accursed handkerchief.

"It's beginning to lighten towards the south."

"Does that mean the rain is going to stop soon?" My voice sounded as strained as his did.

"No. It will probably rain until morning at least." His shoulders stiffened, then sagged, yet he continued to stare fixedly out into the rain. "I apologize for my actions just now. They were ungentlemanly and uncalled-for."

One shameless part of me longed to say that no apologies were needed, that I had enjoyed it as much as he did; such a course would have been not only forward and unladylike, it would have branded me as a shameless hoyden. Any lady worthy of the name probably would have fainted rather than admit even in the most secret recesses of her soul that she enjoyed such sensual wooing.

"Your apology is accepted, Mr. Fordyce." I replied primly.

The conversation died. He doubtless thought me disgraceful for accepting the situation so calmly, and I could not speak for fear my unruly tongue would call him back. We might have sat there for hours like two statues, frozen so by one moment's exploding passion, had it not been for the fire. It had snapped and burned and gobbled up every bit of dry fodder within the hearth before it finally began to flicker in pale death. At last there were nothing but dull coals crouching under a blanket of ash as if to preserve their own warmth.

He had left the chilly draughts of the doorjamb to seek what warmth the fire could offer, yet he had been very careful to take his seat on the other side of the hearth. We had sat in that strained silence, hearing it grow thicker and darker every moment until it was too powerful to be broken by the lightweight weapon of idle chatter.

To me, it was just as well; he had seen how I responded to him. My lack of propriety and delicacy had probably offended him. The thought saddened me immensely.

His face, strongly molded and handsome even in the half dark, was emotionless as he stared into the dying fire. I had watched him covertly from half-closed lids, dropping them whenever he glanced my way, trying to memorize the planes and angles of his face. The struggle of life had taught me to force my body into a semblance of the decorum and propriety expected of a woman of my station, but I had long ago given up the futile exercise of trying to curb my mind.

"The fire's done for." He stood suddenly. "It'll be dark soon and these are as dry as they'll ever get here. We'd best be getting back."

A different guilt washed over me. During our strange, rain-shrouded time in the croft it had been as if the outside world had stood still or had ceased to exist. How selfish I had been to think only of myself and forget that Dougal lay out there in the rain, perhaps injured, perhaps . . ."

"Put this on," Simon ordered and all but flung my dress at me.

I struggled with the still-damp fabric, more conscious of his hulking frame conspicuously staring out at the rain-blurred landscape than of buttons and ties. At last I was decent, though that dress would never be the same; I tried to shake the wrinkles out of the skirt and finally had to settle for the fact that it at least covered my petticoats. My hair was a lost cause, I decided while pulling out the pins. With no mirror it would be impossible to fix it back in even the simplest chignon. Better just to let it hang down my back; after all, I could hardly look worse. I slicked it back as best I could and anchored it behind my ears.

"You look about twelve years old like that," Simon said indulgently. He had reclaimed his coat and once more was the image of a well-to-do country squire rather than a dashing brigand.

"There's no mirror . . ." I replied defensively.

"Don't apologize. It's very attractive."

My fingers shook as I swirled Duncan's old cloak around me. "I wasn't apologizing. Oh, this got completely dry!"

"It won't stay that way for long. It's still raining."

"Are we very far from Jura House?"

"Not very, just a couple of miles."

"Can we walk there before dark?" The idea of

tramping over the rough moor in the shaky light of day was discouraging enough; in the rainy dark without a lantern it was frightening.

He smiled. "We can be there before long, but it'll be dark by then, I'm afraid. Are you ready? I'll get the horses."

"Horses?" My voice had become weak. Until that moment I had kept my mind away from those huge beasts with the uncertain tempers. Once more I was wedged on Pride's back, the ground flying by under his hooves and the spectre of certain death riding beside me . . .

"Of course, horses. Did you think we were going back afoot? Luckily there was enough left of one of the outbuildings to stable them out of the rain . . ."

"I think I'd rather walk . . ."

His hand gently cupped my cheek. He smiled indulgently, without scorn or patronage. "You really are terrified, aren't you?"

"I will not get back on that animal again!"

"I wouldn't ask you to, Mrs. MacLellan. It won't be as comfortable, but do you think you can ride double with me? I assure you, I won't let you fall."

For a moment we soundlessly shared the memory of the first time he had carried me thus, a memory too intimate to be spoken of, and suddenly the world changed. I had no fear of him, which perhaps was foolish, but I could no more fear him than I could myself. Such judgments of the heart are sometimes rash, I knew, yet had he wished my death in the tunnel he would scarcely have made such an effort to rescue me from Pride. For good or ill, I made my decision.

"I know you won't. Just please don't ever expect me to ride anything ever again."

He smiled more widely. "Wait here. I'll bring the horses around."

The rain had slacked off to a thick, persistent drizzle. Pride and Crusader looked uniformly miserable, and I would have sworn that in Pride's questing eye there was a challenge. This time Simon did not carry me up dramatically in his arms, a circumstance I secretly regretted. Instead he lifted me to Crusader's saddlebow with an effortlessness that was a tribute to his strength, then mounted behind me and fitted my body to his. Even with the layers of cloaks and clothing between us, I could feel the warmth of him and lay still in quiet contentment. Pride, his reins securely gripped in Simon's hand, trailed behind. He almost appeared disappointed.

Duncan's old cloak lacked a hood, leaving my face bare to the soft, wet air. After the dubious warmth of the fire, it was even more chilly outside and I squirmed, trying to pull the cloak in tighter.

"Comfortable?"

"Under the circumstances."

He chuckled. "Witch. Do you always give such double-edged answers?"

"You have rescued me twice, sir," I replied,

enjoying to the full this new and peculiar mood of lighthearted camaraderie that had bloomed between us. "Surely you do not wish me to inflate your self-esteem still further."

He seemed pleased by my saucy answer. "I did have something like that in mind, yes." Then, in quite a different tone, "I'm glad you have forgiven me. I hadn't meant it to be like that."

Surely he could hear the erratic thudding of my heart giving the lie to my composed exterior. How dreary it was that ladies were supposed to be pure vessels with no emotions save those of gratitude and mother-love; or was it perhaps that at heart I was no true lady?

"Meant what to be like that?" It was not what I had intended to say. I had thought of a cool and ladylike reply, but my rebellious lips refused to form it.

"My first wooing of you. Surely you have noticed that I . . ." Here he hesitated most maddeningly. ". . . I find you attractive."

"Hardly," I replied with a coquetry heretofore alien to me. "Tell me about it."

"Minx! I shall do no such thing. If you refuse to feed my self-esteem, I fear I must equally starve yours."

Beneath my head his shoulder was sturdy, the arm that held me close, hard with muscles; I felt more secure and protected than ever before in my life. Then why was there a nagging voice in the back of my mind, jeering that I had never been so attractive as since becoming an heiress?

Again my impulses got the better of rational thought. "Did you know there was a priest's hole in Jura House?"

"What on earth made you think of that? I have heard of a secret room or two, but there are always tales like that about old houses. Jura House was built during a time of instability; I suppose it would be surprising if it didn't have something like that. I know the Castle has several."

Surely he would not speak so casually of the matter if he had known anything of my plight, I rationalized. Somehow it seemed very important that every last bit of lingering suspicion be crushed.

"This room is on the upper floor," I said slowly, "and there are endless steps leading down past the ground floor to a tunnel that leads to a rocky scree just below the garden."

"How did you find this out?" His voice was oddly tight.

"I was knocked over the head and put in the priest's hole. Whoever did it left me a lamp so I could find my way out. I couldn't figure out how to open the door to the hallway, but the door leading to the tunnel was ajar . . ." I could feel his muscles tensing. "I crawled out. Apparently the tunnel hasn't been used in years . . . I was afraid it would come down around my ears."

"You could have been killed," he said in a

strained voice. He was affected by my dry narrative, yet he offered no cloying platitudes, for which I was grateful. "Mrs. Wright said something about your having been locked in an upstairs room, but I didn't know . . ."

"I thought Mrs. Docherty would have told you . . ."It slipped out before I could think.

"So you think Mrs. Docherty is in your house as a spy? I'm sorry to disillusion you, but no matter what your family tells you, I do not need to sink to the level of planting informants. You should have stayed put and screamed," he said bluntly.

"I thought of that, but I wasn't sure if the person who attacked me was still about, or even if I was still in Jura House."

"You thought you might be in the Castle?" He was quick!

"It did cross my mind."

"I'm not surprised. Your brother-in-law bears me no love at all, and I'm not sure the aunts don't believe I conceal horns and a pointy tail." He looked down at me. The rain had beaded on his face as it probably had on mine and the colorless sky had turned the blue of his eyes to murky grey. "Do you believe I had anything to do with it?"

"No . . ."

"You say that reluctantly."

"It's difficult. You see, in the middle of the tunnel, right where I couldn't possibly miss it against the dark ground, was one of your initialed handkerchiefs."

His roar of rage so startled the horses that for the next few moments he was fully taken up with calming them. It was strange, yet atop that twisting and plunging animal I felt no fear as long as Simon held me. Surely I could not be so wrong in my judgment?

"Now, suppose you repeat that," he said, when at last everything was calm once more and we were again on our way back to Jura House.

"I said I found one of your initialed handkerchiefs in the tunnel."

His look at me was indescribable. I could all but feel myself melting to a jelly. "Do you believe that I had anything to do with it?"

"No," I replied easily. "You aren't a stupid man, Simon Fordyce. I cannot see you doing anything so foolish as to leave a panel open if you wished it shut, or being so criminally forgetful as to leave one of your monogrammed handkerchiefs behind where I would have to be blind not to see it. It does not take a great intelligence to see this was just a clumsy trick to try to incriminate you."

"I am flattered that you believe so in my innocence, but listen to me, Linnet!" Once again he slipped into the familiarity of my given name as naturally as if he had used it forever. "You must not go back to that house! I don't understand what's going on, but there is danger for you there. I'll take you back to the Castle and send word right away that you're all right . . ."

"Simon . . ." His name came less easily to my tongue, for in saying it I defied both convention and propriety. "No. I must go back to Jura House."

"Why? I guarantee no one will hurt you at the Castle," he growled. "If you like, the MacLellans can visit you freely, but at least I'll know that you will be safe."

How could I tell him that I would not be safe at the Castle, that the greatest danger there would be myself? Ghosts and ghoulies and hobgoblins faded into insignificance against the fearful struggle with my own desires.

"No, Simon. I cannot hide. This thing must be settled."

"Thing?"

"I can think of no other word. The inheritance and how it will be disbursed are the real problems here." I spoke slowly, choosing my words with care. "If that matter were settled, the rest would go away."

"And have you reached a decision?" Beneath my cheek his muscles jumped to a new tautness. I could see his jawline harden almost to a knife edge.

"Yes, one that I think will be the best for the people of the valley."

He was all but holding his breath now. "Well, you saucy wench, are you going to keep me in suspense, or must I begin guessing?"

"I can't get those starving children out of my mind, Simon. The aunts' dream of vanished glories,

Dougal's hope of a squiredom, your vision of an industrialized paradise . . . there are good arguments for each of these, but I can't forget those children's eyes! They are the real MacLellan inheritance, and I must do what I think is best for them."

Simon must have sensed a victory, for he glanced down at me with a warm smile. Above us the sky had darkened to a charcoal color; I had no way of telling if the storm were renewing itself or if time were just moving on through the early winter evening. As long as Simon was there to protect me, I didn't really care.

"I think that is what Duncan had in mind when he left the ordering of it to you, so you could do what he dreamed."

"Only he died before he could tell me," I said. Never far behind, guilt struck at me with pincers of mortification. My husband was dead but a short time, and here I was all but acting the harlot with another man. How ashamed I ought to feel! "I feel rather like Paris and the golden apple."

"Very good analogy," he responded sagely. "One golden prize and three claimants, each with justification. You are extremely well read, my dear."

Though it was a common term of the most casual address, the blandishment sent small shivers down my backbone. "Can a manuscript copyist be less?"

Simon roared with laughter at that. "Oh, Linnet! What did I do before you? Now I cannot stand the suspense any longer . . . Can you tell me your master plan, or is it something you must keep quiet?"

Proudly I recited my plan. "I think the valley needs the mill, Simon. The land is too poor for profitable farming, and fertilizing it is a gamble. My proposition is to give you the land for the mill and to work out an equitable investment where half the mill would belong to you and half to the MacLellans. If there is not enough ready cash for such a scheme, I am sure that there are bankers in Glasgow or Edinburgh who will advance a loan against the land until the mill begins to pay its way . . ."

His silence had not been the attentive silence of a respectful listener. As it had grown harder and more stony, I had talked faster and faster, as if the unalloyed force of my words would convince him of whatever their content lacked. At last I ran dry and the only sound between us was the faraway rumble of thunder, like a giant snoring in its sleep.

"Do you think I would be partners with a man like Dougal MacLellan?" Simon Fordyce snarled. "I'll see him in Hell first!"

Chapter 18

It was full dark by the time we reached Jura House. Simon Fordyce's outburst had led to a short but pungent argument in which I challenged his motives and in turn he questioned my sanity. Dougal was apostrophized as a petty tyrant from another age who wished to set himself up as head of a fiefdom; Simon raged that he had no intention of risking his idea and his capital in a venture with someone who wanted nothing more than to see it fail. I argued that I would be the one in control, and that we had much more to lose than he if it did fail. We were so far gone in heated dispute that no amount of rational logic could have convinced us of either case. Finally there fell between us a hostile silence.

I wished there had been a more concrete barrier between us. It was difficult to lie snuggled so intimately against a man with whom one had just argued and who had come very near to wooing one just for the property one controlled. I felt rather soiled and used. Even the danger and discomfort of being aboard Pride would have been infinitely superior for my self-esteem—if not my nerves—to being so close to a man who, for all his flaws, still excited me unbearably. I sat stiffly, trying to create as much distance between our bodies as possible within his iron grip.

Golden apple, indeed! I thought in some disgust. I had almost made the same mistake as Paris did in giving it to Aphrodite, for by choosing love he caused the Trojan War. Giving in to love seemed to be a common human failing, but I would be different. Of the other two claimants—Hera, the Goddess of the Hearth, and Athena, the Goddess of Wisdom—there must be a superior choice. My offering would be to Athena then, along with a fervent prayer for wisdom. There would be no Trojan War in this valley!

I had just made my allegorical decision when we turned into the yard of Jura House. Under the deep shadows of the trees we were invisible, even if in the unlikely event one of the crowd turned around. The yard seemed full of people, all carrying torches that blazed fitfully, giving the scene an eerie light.

Dougal stood by the doorway, and even before we got close enough to hear his words, his posture alone convinced me of the anger with which he harangued the crowd. He did not look well. Under the best of circumstances, his pale and bruised face, adorned with scrapes and a rakish bandage around the temple, would have been startling; under the flaring torchlight, it was dramatic. His left arm reposed in a sling and he seemed to be standing with some difficulty. All in all, the effect was one that would give a maiden heart a thrill of adoring sympathy, rather as when it had been the fashion for the young ladies of London to go and watch the wounded young men being brought back from the Crimea, under the charitable guise of distributing nosegays.

It was sad for both Dougal and me that at the moment my heart was as hard as any mythological apple of gold.

". . . so I'm depending on you." Dougal's voice was strong, yet with an affecting tremolo of emotion. Even from here, I could see the strain writ on his face. "Mrs. MacLellan is out there somewhere . . . Please find her for me. I . . ." His voice faltered. "I don't see how she can be alive, but we've got to try. If she's lying out there hurt or . . . or . . ."

Here his voice faded away and he staggered a little, as if the effort of standing were becoming too much for him. There was a supportive murmur from the crowd. Now I could see that there weren't as many as had seemed at first, perhaps fifteen or twenty. Beneath his breath Fordyce murmured "Masterly." It was not a compliment.

"We've got to find her, men. She was my brother's wife . . ." Dougal's voice betrayed a touching richness of emotion that should have had nothing to do with that relationship. "Find her for me. Please. Bring her body home . . ." Here his voice broke. My heart went out to him, for at that moment he was so like Duncan, so gentle and vulnerable.

Simon Fordyce snorted and started to walk the horses through the knot of men, which parted like the Red Sea before Moses. I prayed as I had never prayed before that Simon would keep back those acid comments I knew were bubbling just behind his tightly clamped lips. There was a gasp from the crowd as the torchlight fell on our faces.

"I think I can save you all that trouble," he said easily, stopping Crusader before Dougal.

"Linnet!" Dougal breathed in a voice little more than a gurgle. Under the flickering light his face looked ghastly. Then, stronger, "What is the meaning of this? What have you done to her?"

Simon swallowed heavily, but his voice was calm enough. "Saved her life. You should know better than to put a novice on a horse like Pride for her first riding lesson . . ."

The tension between the two men was as tangible as a cold draught. Beyond them there was a muttering among the men like a slight swell in a thickening sea.

"Mrs. MacLellan! Oh, the Lord be praised! "The mood shattered under the assault of Mrs. Docherty and her daughters. They rushed from the house, all babbling words of praise and welcome, sounding the first note of joy to my resurrection. Willie Campbell stepped forward and lifted me from the saddle. His face was alight with happiness, but I heard threatening murmurs beyond in the crowd. Suddenly I knew that Simon was in danger and that it would be up to me to save him.

"Hello, Mrs. Docherty, girls . . . Thank you, Willie. Dougal, are you all right? You look awfully pale. How badly are you hurt?" I babbled on in a loud voice, trying to lay a veneer of normality over what was rapidly becoming a nightmare situation.

"I'm fine," he said through stiff lips. He still looked at me as if not quite convinced that I was mortal. From the way his eyes glittered I suspected that he had a fever; the sooner I could end this performance and get him tucked in bed, the better it would be for everyone.

"Willie, would you please take Pride to the stables and see to him? He's had a rough afternoon, too."

Keep smiling! I told myself sternly through fear that twisted at me with icy claws. I wanted nothing more than a hot supper and a warm bed. Suddenly I was so weary that the thought of climbing the stairs was too exhausting to contemplate, but there was still so much to be done and I the only person to do it.

Stepping forward, I kissed Dougal's rigid cheek. It was cold. The torchlight turned the clustered faces looking toward us into feral night creatures. A flow of angry emotion as palpable as a dark tide flowed through the assemblage. I could almost smell a mounting desire for the release of violence.

"I want to thank you for your efforts in my behalf," I said, raising my voice to be sure that no one misunderstood. "It is comforting to know that had I needed it, you would have come for me. I know that there is bad feeling between some of you and Mr. Fordyce, but without his rescue and aid I would probably be dead at this very moment. For that I am grateful. I do not wish any harm to befall him." Here I was almost shouting.

There was a ripple of sound through the crowd, but the knot of men grudgingly parted enough to give Simon a clear path back to the road. To my surprise it was Simon who seemed angry.

"I do not need your protection," he snapped with stung pride. "Or your patronage, or your partnership!"

I slipped my arm through Dougal's good one in an act of defiance. It lay like wood against mine. "Good evening, Mr. Fordyce. I thank you for your assistance, but I do not think we will meet again." It was the most painful thing I had ever said, each word as if ripped from living tissue.

His eyes shot blue fire. It would not be hard to imagine him doing physical violence.

"Linnet Hudson MacLellan, you are without a doubt the most maddening female ever sent to plague a man, but I tell you one thing . . . I will see you again and I will build that mill!" His voice was like a thunderclap. Then with a swirl of hooves and a half-heard string of oaths he was gone, leaving the dramatically lit yard little more than a flat painted set for a tawdry play.

How wonderful to be a delicate thing of airs and graces who can evade every trying situation by fainting at will. Being both sturdy and self-sufficient, I could resort to no such escape, and so have a fairly clear memory of the rest of that deadly evening.

I remember dismissing the men with more thanks and yet another order that peace must be maintained. I remember taking a strangely quiet Dougal inside and thinking that he must be worse hurt than he was letting on. I remember especially the aunts, for this was their first display of genuine affection for me. Miss Jessie, ever the tender-hearted, embraced me with tears and loving phrases, but it was Miss Agatha's slight pat on my arm accompanied by a dry phrase of concern that touched me the most. Coming from her, it was an unprecedented show of emotion and acceptance. She did care what happened to me, and that alone almost made me break down.

I remember the flurry of activity. The aunts took charge of Dougal themselves, refusing to let me help. Perhaps they had begun to fear the ungodly and unlawful affection that sometimes springs between persons situated as Dougal and I were, but they did not mention it, and I could not.

Mrs. Docherty and her girls took charge of me as if I had been a rag doll or backward child. Ruthlessly I was washed and fed and tucked into bed without having to expend any effort of my own. That was a good thing, for under the soporific effect of the warm water and hot food and their harmless chatter I dissolved into a weak creature capable only of sleep. Vaguely I remember being tucked into my bed, which had been newly made with fresh sheets that smelled of dried lavender, then Mrs. Docherty touchingly favored me with a motherly nighttime benediction the like of which I had not known since before my own mother's last illness.

I do not remember the candle being extinguished, but when I abruptly awoke the room was dark. Clouds still shrouded the dying moon, masking her light, and the blackness of my room was as palpable as a blanket. I awoke suddenly with pounding heart and heaving breath, as if rushing into wakefulness to save myself from some sleep-terror, but I carried no memory of a bad dream.

Then the fabric of the world as I had known it ripped asunder, and I knew what it was that had pulled me into fearful waking.

Footsteps approached my bed. There was the soft scrabbling of hands as they groped their way across the coverlet seeking me. I opened my mouth to scream, but the sound died unborn in my throat at the intruder's whispered words.

"There you are . . . *Rara Avis.*"

Rara Avis is a not uncommon Latin phrase meaning merely rare bird, but it struck a superstitious terror into me. Since "linnet" is also the name of a small songbird, in a moment of the romantic foolishness common to young lovers,

Duncan had christened me his *Rara Avis*. It had become a nickname reserved for our moments of utmost intimacy as man and wife, a loveword known only to the two of us.

"Duncan?"

Now the groping hands had found me. They felt their way up my body until two strong hands bound my shoulders in a grip that was profoundly corporeal.

"Rara Avis" he repeated. "What an obstacle you have become . . ."

Then a blackness more profound than the night fell over me, and I knew no more.

Chapter 19

A t least I was sure I wasn't dead. One couldn't hurt this much and be dead. There were sharp rocks and hard ground beneath me. My mouth was stretched painfully wide and bound with a great deal of foul cloth. My hands and feet were in that painful state past numbness. I was alive, but at the moment, it was poor consolation.

High above, a weak sun sent rays to probe the darkness of my prison, digging glittering fingers into my eyes. I was parched with thirst, and as memory gradually filtered through the discomfort, beset with questions.

First of all, where was I?

I struggled into a sitting position, a task that sounds much easier than it was. Rough stone walls, a debris- and dung-mottled floor, the ghost of a roof . . . This was another ruined croft, but that was no help. The countryside was dotted with them, poor memorials to dreams gone sour.

I strained to cry out, but managing against the gag and my dry throat to produce only a whimper. It would have been so comforting to let go and cry. That, however, would have been nothing but an emotional waste of time and energy. By the position of the sun it must already be past noon; the alarm must have been given hours ago and a search party raised, but they could pass within feet of me and bound like this I could not signal to them.

To spare my readers' sensitivities I will gloss over my struggles to attain freedom. By the time I had succeeded in removing the bonds from my wrists, not only was my skin chafed raw, but I had also sustained several nasty scratches from the rough stone against which I had rasped the rope to fray it. To remove the cloth clotting my mouth was sheer heaven, but the balm of water would have to wait until the painful process of sensation returning to my hands and legs was complete enough to allow me to stand.

During that long time my mind was active, and with a subject no less painful than my extremities. Who had come into my room the night before? Who had done this to me? Who could possibly call me *Rara Avis?*

Duncan was dead! I had seen his poor, mangled body myself, and seen it buried in a churchyard hundreds of miles away. I was not yet in a position to believe in the return of the dead, but . . . My mind swung in angry circles. Could it be possible that Duncan had somehow survived, his mind as shattered as his body, and had come home in some bizarre scheme of some sort? No . . . No, never. Not Duncan.

The sun slid into afternoon, and whatever

frail warmth it had shed now faded. I was still clad in my nightrail, though it had suffered severe damage even before my efforts to free myself.

Ghosts? Malignant spirits? No. If I started believing in those, I might as well admit to madness.

But . . .

Dougal had been injured in his accident; I had seen his arm in a sling myself, yet there had been two strong arms on my attacker the night before, and no injured man could have shifted my bulk from Jura House to here. And Dougal could not know about the intimate joke of *Rara Avis;* neither could Simon Fordyce. That was the worst point, for it had been a secret between Duncan and me. Without that, there were any number of candidates for the position of villain, but . . .

But! Always but!

My head hurt. I was thirsty and hungry and cold. Feeling had returned to my limbs with a vengeance, seemingly determined to make up for the time spent numb. If I didn't do something quickly I would be destined to spend a night in the dubious protection of this ruined building. That was not an attractive prospect, but it was another, even less appealing thought that finally got me moving, without heed to the rough ground beneath my bare feet.

Whoever had placed me there would sooner or later come back.

At last, thanks more to the charity and

guidance of our beneficent Creator than to any skill or knowledge of my own, I finally found myself on the back path that used to run between the Castle and Jura House, just as the last pale smudges of light were leaving the sky. Outside the croft, I had followed the sound of water to a sluggish burn where I had slaked my thirst with the peaty-tasting water, then searched the wild country blindly for any familiar sign. The sight of Jura House at last, its windows ablaze with light, was the most beautiful thing I had ever seen.

The yard was full of horses. With a slight thrill I recognized the black bulk of Crusader. That meant that Simon was there, and my treacherous heart gave a small leap despite the tense parting of the day before.

Ah, Vanity! Learned moralists and theologians have lectured fulsomely against its pernicious influence; how much I could have been spared had I stopped to give heed to their wise counsel.

My hair was wild and studded with debris from the floor where I had lain and from the clutching woods where I had walked; my gown was still an intimate garment in which I should have been embarrassed to be seen even had it not been stained and ripped; I was filthy as well as bleeding in at least a dozen places . . .

The curtains to the sitting-room window had not been drawn; it was a French-style window that had more of the attributes of a door. I stood in the dark before entering, hesitating to expose myself in such a condition, and in so hesitating, was lost.

The room was full of sound. Even though the window was almost completely closed, I could hear the bull-like roar that was Simon's contrasting with the shrill eagle's cry that was Dougal's. There was a third man there, a very authoritative, mustachioed older gentleman who had the carriage and bearing that demands respect.

"You dare come to this house again!" Dougal shrieked. His face was nearly as pale as the bandage that encircled his head. "I should have you horsewhipped!"

"You're welcome to try," was Simon's growled reply. "But not until you tell me where Linnet is!"

"How dare you call her Linnet! What sort of dirty games have you two *parvenus* been playing?"

Here the older man started, his face mottled with anger and mustache twitching as if he would speak, but Simon held up an imperious hand and he remained still.

"Ever since she duped my brother into marriage, she has caused this family nothing but heartbreak and shame," Dougal ranted on. "Carrying on with you like a trollop, cozening my poor brother into writing that damnable will, betraying the trust that is the sacred duty of every MacLellan . . . Even running away to be with you in the night like a woman of the streets!"

A muscle in Simon's cheek jumped as if it had

a life of its own. "And what makes you say that?" His voice was deadly quiet.

"A note. She left a note saying she was leaving to be with you . . ."

"Are you quite sure of that?" asked Mr. Cameron. He had been on the big sofa and out of my line of vision. I had almost forgotten what the solicitor looked like, having seen him only at the emotional moment of the will reading, but I did not remember him as being so grim looking. "May we see that note?"

"Just because you are his creature does not give you the right to doubt my word," said Dougal haughtily. "That little whore has run away to join him, and be damned to her!"

The room erupted then into a cacophony of shouts, with Simon having to be physically restrained from striking Dougal's angry, supercilious face. It would have been the perfect time for me to step forward and refute his bitter calumny, had not my arms been suddenly pinioned behind me in a cruel grip and a rough hand clamped across my mouth. I had a fleeting glimpse of a vaguely familiar face belonging to one of Dougal's satellites. It was contorted with hatred.

It was too much; I did faint then, as much from surprise as from exhaustion. My last conscious memory was of Simon most gratifyingly saying that he would search the country until he found me and call out the militia if necessary.

* * * * *

He slapped me once, hard, and then again on the other cheek. And again. And again.

My eyelids were heavy; it took a concentrated effort to open them.

"Good," he said. There was a maniacal light in his eyes. One hand firmly gripped the collar of my ravaged nightgown; the other descended again to my face, making the scar feel like a brand. "I should hate for you to miss out on your end!"

The watery lamplight gleamed dully on his golden hair.

"Dougal?" I forced out between bruised lips. "Duncan? In God's name, who are you?"

His crow of laughter echoed weirdly in the little room. "So you wouldn't have known! How much did you care for your husband, anyway? Just enough to gain control of his property . . . all that should have been mine? My God, Linnet, you have been a devil sent from Hell to torment me!"

At least one thing was solved. "Dougal, I don't understand . . ."

"Don't lie to me!" Once more his hand struck my flesh. "You've taunted me and mocked me and ridiculed me . . . Dangling in front of me that which was mine by the right of succession, and then snatching it away because of some silly will . . . If it hadn't been for you I would have had everything!"

Finally my brain was beginning to work again. "You killed Duncan!"

"Yes! Yes, I did, and I'm proud of it! He would have perverted the sacred rights of the MacLellans! He was going to let that devil Fordyce build his damned mill; he was going to let someone else take over the proper place of the MacLellans! It wasn't fair that he should inherit, not if he was going to give away all that was ours! I should have inherited . . . been hereditary leader of the valley . . . Duncan—your precious, mewling Duncan—wasn't fit to be a MacLellan! He didn't understand the land, the power of the land . . ." His voice had drifted off into a croon, as if he were speaking of a lover.

"It's all your fault, you know," Dougal went on in a surprisingly ordinary tone. "If he hadn't gone so foolish about you, there wouldn't have been any problem. Poor Duncan would have met with an accident in London, and as his loving brother, I should have brought his body home. But there was you . . . and you wouldn't die!

"You must be part cat, Linnet, rather than a bird, to have so many lives. I had hoped that you would go back to London after your telegram 'got lost,' but you knew what a sweet thing you had going and you came on . . ."

"I didn't know . . . I just wanted a home and a family . . ." I moaned. He had released me now, but I lay like a puddle of boneless jelly on the gritty flagged floor.

"Even when I ran you down, you wouldn't die, and of all the cursed luck, Fordyce found you and saved your life." He was pacing around me like a hungry animal. "I didn't dislike you, really I didn't," he murmured and stroked my hair with a terrible travesty of a lover's caress. "I didn't mind your being here, or playing housewife. It was fun to watch you make that old witch Agatha mad. If you had agreed to hand control of what was mine over to me, I would have let you live here and clean and scrub all you liked.

"But no!" His voice had risen to a roar that bounced from wall to wall like sharp pebbles. "You had to act as if you knew what was best for the valley. You—a guttersnipe from London—telling me about the MacLellan obligations! I could have killed you then . . . I tried, but you wouldn't die!" Now it shrilled to a frustrated squeal.

"To what Dark Power did you pray, Linnet? What evil force protected you? You almost caught us, you know. We meet here." His gesture encompassed the bare little room. "This is the second priest's hole. It was revealed to me so that I could restore the glory of the valley, so that the MacLellans could take their rightful place again . . . I'm not the only one; there are men loyal to the MacLellans, men who can't be bought with money. They helped me . . . Ah, it was such fun! We burned crops and barns and killed animals, and then the next morning I would shake my head sorrowfully when Fordyce was blamed."

His laugh was an obscenity. "I even burned his once, just for spite, and pretended it was a righteous uprising of an outraged peasantry. It didn't make him leave, though . . . Why didn't you believe that it was he who locked you in the priest's hole upstairs?"

I listened to his ranting in a daze. Here were the answers I had sought, spilling forth in a sick, triumphant babble, though I was almost certain that I should never have the opportunity to tell anyone. Until now I had been protected by blind luck, but I could not get rid of the queasy sensation that I had no more luck left. He was going to kill me, and I could do nothing to stop him.

"Pride . . ." I said suddenly. "You planned for him to kill me. You weren't hurt at all . . . You deliberately made your horse act up, and then fell off!"

"I had to protect myself, didn't I?" His tone was frighteningly reasonable. "I thought I played the role of worried, injured brother rather well."

"You can't kill me," I cried. "How will you explain it?"

"Linnet, Linnet . . . you're just like Duncan. Both of you underestimated me! Flexibility is the key. I had planned to have everyone think you had run away with Fordyce—you'd like that, wouldn't you, you little whore? Then when your bones were found out on the moors, with any luck at all he'd be blamed for your murder! But you came back, like some sort of accursed cat! This time I'll be sure you're dead, though it rushes me. I can't wait now for someone to stumble across you on the moors. Your remains will be found in the ruins of Jura House."

That was what was bothering me! For the last few minutes something had been nagging at the edge of my attention, but under the circumstances I had paid the matter little mind. Now I knew it was the ever-thickening smell of smoke.

"Fire?" I could not keep a quiver of fear out of my voice.

"Fire. Cleansing fire. Purifying fire." It was a religious statement and his eyes–suddenly so different from Duncan's eyes–glowed with a fanatical fervor.

"But you said I had run away to join Fordyce! How can I be found here?" I was screaming now, trying to find some chink in his horribly tight plan.

"Tragic . . . you came back for your clothes, or perhaps Fordyce rejected you . . . no one will ever know, or believe anything he says. You were upstairs when the fire broke out and no one will know you were there until we sift through the ruins. It is perhaps a bit melodramatic to sacrifice the house, especially after all the work you've put into it, but sometimes extreme measures are the best. And I will have the satisfaction of knowing that at last you are really dead!"

He smiled angelically. "'I promise to grieve for you most properly. Maybe even a window in the church in memory of you and Duncan; that would be a nice touch, don't you think?"

"You're mad," I cried in frustration, but it was a lie. The meanderings of a lunatic would have been easier to bear, but Dougal MacLellan was extremely intelligent and utterly sane.

"Hardly, dear sister. You brought all this down upon yourself. As a matter of fact, I am something of a hero. It was I who found the fire and risked life and limb to arouse the household. In fact, at this very moment I am making a last-minute check of the house to be sure everyone is out before I stagger outside and collapse dramatically. What a pity no one knew you were here. There won't be any accusations, that would be a vulgarity beneath a MacLellan, but you can rest assured that your lover Fordyce will be blamed for the fire. He will not dare stay in the valley then."

"And still you lose," I screamed, and swayed to my feet. Had there been a visible door I could have been fighting toward it, but this was a plain box just like the other priest's hole. "If I die, you lose everything . . . you aren't my closest kin! You've forgotten my grandfather . . . He'll inherit!"

An expression of angry distaste crossed his features. The room was filling with smoke, thin, lazy tendrils swirling like fog. "How could I forget him, when that upstart Fordyce paraded him in front of me tonight? Pushy old man . . . Your family really has no breeding, Linnet."

I stared at him with wide eyes. That military-looking old man, my grandfather? It was not hard to accept that he might have been a general, but the look of worried concern on his face and the way he had reacted to Dougal's insults did not fit my conception of the man who had cut his daughter off completely so many years ago. Besides, how did he get here, and why?

Dougal hadn't stopped talking. "It was sheer folly on Duncan's part to mix our blood with yours. Future generations should thank me for saving them that taint. After all, MacLellan breeding is equal to that of any in the land, including those upstart Germans who call themselves Royal!

"As for your grandfather, he will get nothing. When I think of how close I came to killing you before finding out about him . . . before providing the correct legal safeguards . . . Careless! Careless! You see, Linnet, planning is so important. You left a will, you know, a will you did not have time to change before you went to join your lover, leaving everything to me, as your dear husband wanted you to. As it should have been from the beginning!"

"A will . . . My signature in the Bible! You forged it."

His smile was jaunty. "No, but close enough. I am unskilled in such artistic endeavors, but there is an engraver in Edinburgh who sometimes obliges me . . . We have worked together before on certain manners pertaining to financial advancement . . ."

Even as I fought off paralyzing fright and the encroaching smoke to seek an answer that could convince him of the folly of his plan, I was forced to admit it was masterly. He had overlooked nothing.

I was doomed.

Looking disturbingly like a teatime guest who is afraid of missing another appointment, Dougal took one last look around.

"I'm sorry I have to leave you now, but I think I should go; if I stay much longer they might send in someone looking for me. You can scream if you like, but no one will hear you. Fires are notoriously noisy things. Breathe deeply when the smoke becomes thick," he added confidingly. "That way you'll probably be dead before the flames reach you. It would be a much pleasanter death. Oh, and to help you pass the time, I'll leave the lamp. You might want to spend your last minutes looking through Duncan's things." He gestured toward the corner where the black case with tan straps sat.

Facing certain death affects one in ways never dreamed of; I became very angry. I had accepted the fact that I should not get out of there alive, but I had also determined that if I were to die, he should join me.

Screaming something along that order, I flung myself at him, vaguely intending to hold him down until the smoke overcame us both, but I had overestimated my strength and underestimated his. His weakened appearance had been due more to superb acting together with shock at seeing me alive and well the night before than to injury; save for a few superficial scrapes, he had been unhurt in his carefully planned fall. With insulting ease, he flung me against the opposite wall with stunning impact, then opened the door to a roiling cloud of smoke.

"By the by, I've jammed the door catch. It's broken, but then it will never need to be opened again. Good-bye, Linnet." He clapped a handkerchief to his mouth and was gone.

I flung myself against the blank wall where the door had been, beating against the wood in a senseless frenzy until my hands were raw, and screaming like a madwoman. The smoke was thicker now, rasping at my throat. I couldn't think so clearly anymore, except to realize that this final time he had won. I was dead, as dead as the legendary priest who had supposedly starved rather than betray his hiding place. In a moment of superstitious terror I searched the shadows to see if his desiccated bones shared my tomb, but my only companions were Duncan's belongings.

The air was going bad. The lamp flame shivered and shrank. By turning it out, I could save enough air for a few more minutes of life, but I could not gather the courage to spend my last moments in the dark.

Curiosity, they say, is the besetting sin of a woman. I had to know. By now I could no longer stand, so I crawled to the corner where Duncan's case sat and solved yet another mystery. Neatly folded on top sat my missing handkerchiefs, and with one of the queer skips of intellect which the brain sometimes makes, I knew why. My first day here, Simon Fordyce had loaned me a handkerchief, which I had forgotten to return. In hopes of incriminating Simon, Dougal had taken the handkerchief, but could not risk taking just that one, in case I should remember. He had played that little game with my Bible, too, either from sheer meanness or to cast doubt on my credibility. With sudden clarity, I understood. He had wanted a sample of my handwriting; even that early, he had been considering my death. There was none of my writing in Mother's Bible, however, and he had been forced to let me sign the family Bible. How it must have galled him to know that my name would be enshrined in that list of dead MacLellans . . .

It was with trepidation that I opened Duncan's case, fearing a wash of pain and guilt on seeing his things once more. There was sadness, yes, but even touching the robe that had been my wedding present to him evoked no emotional response. *How dreadful*, I thought, *to have to meet my Maker with the knowledge that not only was I a failure but that even my marriage had been a sham.*

I would have read Duncan's diary then to find out what he really had wanted to do for the valley, thinking that one sin more could hardly count against me in such circumstances, but the air was thick and black and swirling . . . It was too dark to read now; I'd just hold onto the diary until it got lighter . . .

A queer jumble of thoughts filled my mind. It is with some shame as a Christian woman that I admit my last thoughts were not of the imminent meeting with my Redeemer, nor of the Last Judgment that would soon be meted out to me, but rather a sad regretfulness that I should never be able to tell Simon Fordyce how very much I loved him.

With Duncan's diary clutched so tightly to my chest that it later had to be prized by force out of my grip, I laid my head down and prepared to die.

Chapter 20

How long ago that all seems! At first the nightmares of fire terrorized me, bringing me screaming from sleep; then my beloved husband would soothe me until I was calm again. Simon never complained about his interrupted slumbers, for he too had such dreams, terrible dreams that he would not be able to rescue me in time or that Miss Jessie had been wrong.

Yes, dear fuddly Miss Jessie had seen the secret door to the second priest's hole; it was she who told Simon where I was, even as her own nephew cursed her for a traitor. Simon did not falter. He wrapped himself in a water-soaked blanket and entered the blazing hulk of Jura House to find me. The tale of how Simon rescued me that dreadful night rapidly passed into local lore; even after all this time one can still hear greatly exaggerated versions of it in the valley.

I suppose it was this old story that intrigued Angus, our oldest son. He is a wonderful young man, and the image of his father. It is at his urging that I am examining those dreadful days again in such painful detail. For some reason or other, Angus has taken it into his head to write a book about our family and the history of the Fordyce Mill. I cannot imagine why; we are really just ordinary people.

Nearly all those who were here during those days of fear are gone now. The tales of that unhappy time have become so wild I have decided that if Angus is to write the story, he must have the correct version. Perhaps it is pure vanity, but I do wish to protect my reputation if it is to be exposed and laid open to Posterity.

Poor Dougal was hanged; I wish we could comfort ourselves with the idea that he was insane, but it would be an evasion of the truth. He was cruel and calculating and ruthless, but never insane. Desire for power and jealousy of his brother drove him to kill poor Duncan and to try to kill me. He died unrepentant, trying to raise an army of followers even as he stood on the gallows. A sad end for the last of the MacLellan line.

Miss Agatha and Miss Jessie were never the same after the night Jura House burned, poor dears. I never knew exactly what Dougal had been telling them about me and they never volunteered any information, but after he was revealed as the cause of the trouble, they both were so rueful of their treatment of me that I suspected his tales had been far less than savory.

So deep was their chagrin that they even talked of investing their shares of the inheritance and taking rooms in Kilayrnock. My heart melted with pity at such sacrifice, for the lodging places available to their purse would have made Jura House look palatial. I had lived in such circumstances; they had not. I could not allow them to make such a move.

It wasn't fair. They had spent all their lives trying to do what they believed to be right, what they had been taught as children that they should do, only to have their plans and dreams used and distorted by Dougal, who in turn was driven by his own dark visions. I pitied them all.

After much thought and prayer, I decided that my task was done. Duncan had intended me to steward the MacLellan fortune, which I had done to the best of my ability. It really didn't belong to me, but to Miss Agatha and Miss Jessie. After much discussion, Mr. Cameron finally arranged matters to my satisfaction. The mill site and guaranteed access were sold to Simon Fordyce; work was put in hand to rebuilding Jura House as a modern residence where the old ladies could live, if not in splendor, at least in gracious comfort for the rest of their lives. When all was done to my satisfaction, I signed everything back to the aunts, keeping only a small sum for my brideclothes. I brought Simon a very poor dowry, but he didn't care a bit.

Understandably there was some tension and unhappiness after Dougal's death, but as time passed the relationship between the rebuilt Jura House and the Castle became both cordial and pleasant. I did not realize how much the aunts' feelings had changed until years later after both of them passed on to the Heavenly realm and Mr. Cameron announced that they had willed their entire fortune – house, farm, land, money, everything to me.

From that dramatic day of the fire I don't suppose that it ever occurred to anyone that Simon and I would not marry, but even I was surprised by the scandalous haste upon which he insisted. I remember him coming into my bedroom before my injuries from the fire allowed me to leave my bed. Mrs. Docherty was indignant when he chased her out, for it was most improper, but then my darling Simon is very seldom proper.

He insisted that we be wed immediately, and when I protested that my year of mourning for my mother and for Duncan was not yet over, he said, "I mean neither of them any disrespect, my very correct Linnet, but I think neither of them would mind." His voice became husky with emotion. "It's just that I've come so close to losing you. I want the right to love you and protect you the rest of your life. I can't run the risk of losing you again, even for a short time." His arms closed around me tightly, as if defying anyone to oppose him.

What woman could stand up against such blandishments? I could not, and, were the truth told, I didn't try very hard. Immodest as it may have been, I wanted to be his wife with a wild passion that grew and grew each day until I thought I should explode from it.

My grandfather was appalled by our decision. He had hoped that I would finish my year of mourning with him and be married with due ceremony from Finchwood Hall, as my mother should have been. As I got to know him, I actually began to like the old man, gruff and autocratic as he was, though the memories of my mother suffering all those years of want and work made it somewhat difficult. If only she could have been the one to experience this reunion . . .

It was difficult for him, too, I believe, though the old man would have found it profoundly embarrassing to acknowledge his tender emotions. The pride that had ruined his life still held him firmly in its toils; however, I believe that in those years of loneliness he had more than paid for his sins. After my mother eloped with my father, he sat in lonely self-righteousness, missing her dreadfully but unwilling to make the first move. In all those years there was no communication between them, save a short note with no return address, to inform him of my birth.

It is to his credit that after some time had passed he relented and tried to search for us; by that time, however, the intervening years and my father's wandering ways had left a cold trail. As far as the General was concerned, it seemed that we had vanished from the earth. That is how things stood until he heard from Mrs. Morrison.

Dear Mrs. Morrison! Perhaps she was an

unlikely *deus ex machina* for our little drama of estrangement, but she was certainly an efficient one. Unable to get over her fears about my being alone among strangers in an alien land, she had taken matters into her own hands and written to him. Though Grandfather never told me much about that letter, I have little doubt that Mrs. Morrison gave him a sharp piece of her mind. In any case, it was the first news he had had of his family in eighteen years, and to his credit he acted on it instantly, writing to the magistrate of Kilayrnock for help.

The local magistrate was, and is, Simon.

I like to think Grandfather's last years were happy, for despite his opposition to our precipitate marriage, he liked and respected Simon. His last years were spent as much at the Castle as at Finchwood Hall, and he lived long enough to dandle his third great-grandchild on his knee, giving the youngsters the love he had hoarded so long. Adored by the children, his and the old aunts' declining years were full of love and warmth.

Even though I was as anxious to marry Simon as he was to marry me, I could not help remembering Duncan. Dear, sweet Duncan, who shared my life for such a short time but who changed it forever. I had thought I loved him, but until I met Simon Fordyce I had no idea of the real meaning of love, of the sacrifice, the passion, the total involvement of which only true love is capable.

In the end, it was Duncan himself who put my

unquiet mind at ease. With no little qualms, I had finally decided to read the parts of his diary that concerned me. In my last conscious moments in that burning room I had clutched Duncan's diary tightly, so tightly that after the fire my nurses were hard put to prize it from my fingers. The diary confirmed Dougal's boasts, differing only in that Duncan was much more aware of the threat his brother presented than Dougal had imagined. It gave sad testimony as well to Duncan's belief in the intrinsic good of his brother, a tragic mistake that caused Duncan's death. If only he had been more cautious, more watchful . . . And, despite my sorrow, I found my peace of mind.

  . . . *and right now, my Linnet, my Rara Avis, can only think of gratitude as love. I do love her and can only hope that when she comes to fall in love, real love, it will be with me.*

It was Duncan's last gift to me, he who had given so much and to whom I had returned so little. He had given me the freedom to love Simon now.

I still think of Duncan, especially when I look out at the rejuvenated valley and think how proud he would have been of it. In actuality, the mill has changed the valley itself very little, but the lives of the people are immeasurably better. We will never be a rich land, but at least now the spectre of hunger is banished.

After the mill was established, I began a school. The round-cheeked children who trudge there daily bear little resemblance to the starvelings whose hollow eyes so haunted me those first few months.

The land, too, has come to life again. Simon agreed with me that some of the profits from the mill should be put back into the land. As both head of the mill and business manager for the aunts' properties, he could see the need for both in the valley. Our valley will never rival the lushness of the country to the south, yet it feeds our people, and more. With both the mill and the rejuvenated land, the valley folk live better than they have ever done before.

That is not to say that all have accepted the mill; although the relationship between it and the valley is peaceable, it is not always amicable. There are many absences during the lambing season and again during harvest, which makes Simon furious, and complaints from some of the farmers that the mill will not take child labor, a stipulation upon which I insisted and in which Simon humored me. I cannot blame the poor families for wanting to increase their income, but never from the backs of children.

"Are you writing about all that again?" Simon asks, knowing that this is one of my crusades. He is looking over my shoulder—older, greyer, but still erect and just as handsome as he was the dark, cold night he rescued me on the road to Jura House. All these years, and my heart still leaps with love.

"No," I reply. "Just finishing up something I promised Angus."

"For that book he's been working on? Silly stuff. It's all over and done with. You would be much better off with a walk in the garden."

"But I'm . . ." I begin, only to be stopped by the warm gleam in his eyes.

"Then let me say I would be much better for a walk in the garden." He smiles, a smile that still has the power to melt all my resistance. "With you."

He is right, as he is so maddeningly often. The story is over, the past is gone. Only the future is important. And the garden is lovely this time of year.

About the Author

Janis Susan May is a seventh-generation Texan and a third-generation wordsmith who writes mysteries as Janis Patterson, romances and other things as Janis Susan May, children's books as Janis Susan Patterson and scholarly works as J.S.M. Patterson.

Formerly an actress and singer, a talent agent and Supervisor of Accessioning for a bio-genetic DNA testing lab, Janis has also been editor-in-chief of two multi-magazine publishing groups. She founded and was the original editor of The Newsletter of the North Texas Chapter of the American Research Center in Egypt, which for the nine years of her reign was the international organization's only monthly publication. Long interested in Egyptology, she was one of the founders of the North Texas ARCE chapter and was the closing speaker for the ARCE International Conference in Boston in 2005.

Janis and her husband live in Texas with an assortment of rescued furbabies.

www.JanisSusanMay.com
www.JanisPattersonMysteries.com

hollow eyes so haunted me those first few months.

The land, too, has come to life again. Simon agreed with me that some of the profits from the mill should be put back into the land. As both head of the mill and business manager for the aunts' properties, he could see the need for both in the valley. Our valley will never rival the lushness of the country to the south, yet it feeds our people, and more. With both the mill and the rejuvenated land, the valley folk live better than they have ever done before.

That is not to say that all have accepted the mill; although the relationship between it and the valley is peaceable, it is not always amicable. There are many absences during the lambing season and again during harvest, which makes Simon furious, and complaints from some of the farmers that the mill will not take child labor, a stipulation upon which I insisted and in which Simon humored me. I cannot blame the poor families for wanting to increase their income, but never from the backs of children.

"Are you writing about all that again?" Simon asks, knowing that this is one of my crusades. He is looking over my shoulder—older, greyer, but still erect and just as handsome as he was the dark, cold night he rescued me on the road to Jura House. All these years, and my heart still leaps with love.

"No," I reply. "Just finishing up something I promised Angus."

"For that book he's been working on? Silly stuff. It's all over and done with. You would be much better off with a walk in the garden."

"But I'm . . ." I begin, only to be stopped by the warm gleam in his eyes.

"Then let me say I would be much better for a walk in the garden." He smiles, a smile that still has the power to melt all my resistance. "With you."

He is right, as he is so maddeningly often. The story is over, the past is gone. Only the future is important. And the garden is lovely this time of year.

About the Author

Janis Susan May is a seventh-generation Texan and a third-generation wordsmith who writes mysteries as Janis Patterson, romances and other things as Janis Susan May, children's books as Janis Susan Patterson and scholarly works as J.S.M. Patterson.

Formerly an actress and singer, a talent agent and Supervisor of Accessioning for a bio-genetic DNA testing lab, Janis has also been editor-in-chief of two multi-magazine publishing groups. She founded and was the original editor of The Newsletter of the North Texas Chapter of the American Research Center in Egypt, which for the nine years of her reign was the international organization's only monthly publication. Long interested in Egyptology, she was one of the founders of the North Texas ARCE chapter and was the closing speaker for the ARCE International Conference in Boston in 2005.

Janis and her husband live in Texas with an assortment of rescued furbabies.

www.JanisSusanMay.com
www.JanisPattersonMysteries.com